THE HEMINGWAY KITTENS

Borgo Press Books by A. R. Morlan

The Amulet: A Novel of Horror
The Chimera and the Shadowfox Griefer and Other Curious People
Dark Journey: A Novel of Horror
Ewerton Death Trip: A Walk Through the Dark Side of Town
The Fold-O-Rama Wars at the Blue Moon Roach Hotel and Other Colorful Tales of Transformation and Tattoos
The Hemingway Kittens and Other Feline Fancies and Fantasies
Of Vampires & Gentlemen: Tales of Erotic Horror
'Rillas and Other Science Fiction Stories

THE HEMINGWAY KITTENS

AND OTHER FELINE FANCIES AND FANTASIES

A. R. MORLAN

THE BORGO PRESS

MMXIII

THE HEMINGWAY KITTENS

FIRST EDITION

Published by Wildside Press LLC

www.wildsidebooks.com

DEDICATION

To Mary Wickizer Burgess

For all her extraordinary work on this
volume—this book wouldn't exist without her
many, many hours of hard work and
dedication to another's dream—
I cannot thank you enough!

AND

For My Cats, Past, Present, and Even Future—

You keep me going, you've saved my life, and
you've become my life…

CONTENTS

INTRODUCTION
A CAT OF NINE TALES

My very dear late friend, Ardath Mayhar, was one of those individuals who not only nurtured within her an immense literary talent that found expression in her own novels, stories, and poems, but also somehow managed to act as a catalyst for other voices just emerging from their creative chrysalides. She accomplished this partly by providing, in her last decades, private professional editorial advice for a variety of old and new writers.

Hence, when David Feintuch was trying to shape his first novel, *Midshipman's Hope*, into something that might be publishable, she was able to tender some suggestions that helped move that project forward to a successful conclusion.

From my own dealings with her, it was clear that she knew just what to say to the wide range of correspondents and friends who brought so many literary gifts to lay at her feet. She helped make their work better. She helped make *them* better. She was a positive force who accomplished a great deal of good from her self-built metal house in the middle of the East Texas muddle from which she came.

I have no idea how many artists Ardath influenced, but the number seems to grow with my knowledge of the field, with the expansion of my own network of authors and agents and editors.

A.R. Morlan was one of her friends and colleagues way back when, long before I'd encountered either writer—and now I'm privileged to count "A.R." among my *own* dear friends.

This is a woman of enormous talent, whose fiction is utterly without compare among modern American masters. She sees things that no one else sees, she finds connections that no one else has ever imagined, and she makes her prose sing and vibrate with a barely constrained but firmly disciplined power, with immense feeling, with great sympathy for the all-too-human characters who people her literary worlds.

She is, in my estimation, one of those authors who will someday, long after she and I are both gone, be "discovered" by the critics, and acclaimed as a modern master of the short story form. Dissertations will be written about her work, and pundits will nod their heads in affirmation, muttering "Yes, yes." But all that future discussion and all that future popularity will not penetrate even a millimeter into the complexity of her work, the sheer scope and breadth and depth of it. Nor should it.

This collection includes some of my favorite Morlan tales—only because both Mary and I are, quite simply, "animal crackers"—just like A.R. We live for our critters, who return our love with a devotion that none of us can ever imagine. Both cats and dogs have adapted themselves symbiotically to human beings, and one wonders sometimes, in watching them cavort for us, in experiencing the sheer joy of their existence, who is the master here—and who the mastered. Perhaps it signifieth not.

A.R.'s love for her cats is evident in her work—and in her life. Her love for her writing is equally clear. This is what she was meant to do—always. This is who she is—always. Through adversity, through experiences that would have destroying a lesser individual, through pain and sorrow and way too much travail, she has persevered; and what you read in this little volume of tales, what you see in her other collections that Mary and I have edited, synthesizes the essence of that large spirit that has somehow survived the Trials of Job.

I think her cats did it. I really do. I think they appeared to provide her with just what she needed. Alas, Ardath Mayhar is no longer with us to give us solace and advice and love. She did what *she* needed to do—and then she left her corpus of work to remind us of what *we* needed to do.

But it was the cats, the spirits of all the writers and creative folk who've ever lived, who yet remain. Who is the master? Who is the mastered?

Is it the cat of nine tales? *Mirabile dictu!*

—Robert Reginald,
June 6, 2013

FOREWORD

I've noticed that when it comes to writers, there are two basic "types" (in the U.S., at least)—"Hemingway writers" and "Fitzgerald writers." Totally different stylistic approaches, completely incompatible mindsets. Concise, literal, muscular writing vs. slightly rambling, idealized, somewhat feminine prose (and by feminine, I am referring to common traits associated with women in general—increased verbosity, reliance on feelings to establish mood, and so on—not necessarily one's gender *per se*). These two "types" don't make for good co-writers, as I've discovered to my chagrin (and not to mention considerable time wasted on trying to make the would-be partnership work!). Nor do they tend to recommend other writers whose work doesn't in some way mirror or mimic *their* preferred stylistic model. (Which often leaves us "Fitzgerald" types out in the cold when it comes time to get endorsed by the more prevalent "Hemingway" followers!)

I suppose one could compare this schism to the one of "cat people" vs. "dog people"—granted, many folks like both equally, but somewhere down the line, everyone has a favorite…and just as the works of Mr.

Hemingway and Mr. Fitzgerald often appear in the same libraries, so do cats and dogs, but—if one has to make a choice between one or the other, not both, that's when you find out what sort of person one is.

All my life I've been a cat person, and despite the title of this collection (and the story which inspired it), I'm also very much a Fitzgerald writer. Granted, Fitzgerald didn't have cats (he was a dog person), and Hemingway did have them, often in great numbers down in Florida; but I've never been a major fan of his work, despite having read much of it in college English courses (the head English professor of my now defunct college—who recently became defunct himself—was vehemently anti-Fitzgerald, calling him "minor" and "not worth studying," despite the protests of his largely female students, who kept begging him to include at least one Fitzgerald novel in his American Novels course)…and I honestly can say, I cannot remember anything from any of Hemingway's books or short stories! But Fitzgerald—now his prose spoke to me. Just as cats have always "spoken" to me…sometimes positively, sometimes not. But even though not all my cat relationships have ended well, all have been memorable. I hope at least some of these stories might also "speak" to my readers.…

—A. R. Morland & Cats
May, 2013

THE
HEMINGWAY KITTENS

Some people may say that cats and bookstores don't mix, that small beasts with claws and the occasional ability to spray have no place among shelved books which reach from the floor to near-ceiling…but answer me, is there anything more appealing than the sight of a cat curled up next to an opened book? With is softly pointed chin resting on the creamy-white printed pages?

True, initially I began shutting cats up inside my bookstore to take care of a minor mouse problem before it became a multiple mice problem, but after the first time I approached the store minutes before opening time, and saw that small crowd of people standing before the shop's display window, cooing and oohing over the sight of Chatty and Muffin curled up into tiger-and-white commas next to the shiny-covered copies of the latest Stephen King novel, I realized that I was on to something. I hadn't seen people react like that since I'd last been in New York City during the winter holidays, when Macy's set up its annual Christmas window displays—and that had been the year they'd done the *Little Women* scenes, back in 1979.

The connection with the name of the store didn't hurt, either—Barrett and Browning's did have that "couples" connotation, and the fact that Chatty was a she and Muffin was a he (even if he was smaller than she was) only seemed to enhance the store's image. Pretty soon, customers started asking where "Barrett and Browning" were, and if I could coax those two sleepy felines out among the shelves during regular store hours, it usually meant a few extra dollars in the till, especially those small—but expensive—items like bookmarks or protective covers for paperback books... all of which I managed to order in cat designs.

Long after the mouse problem was solved, I still kept cats in my shop. Luckily, Muffin wasn't a sprayer, and neither he nor Chatty was wont to rend their claws along the exposed spines of the shelved books (both the new ones I kept out front, and the used section toward the back of the narrow rectangle of a half-store), so as long as their litter pans were scooped clean, and their bowls of food and water were kept full, my two feline salespeople did their jobs well...so well, in fact, that within a couple of years, I found that I needed help in the store. Initially, Barrett and Browning was little more than a hobby for me; after my husband passed away, I'd leased the building with my insurance money, knowing full well that I'd never really be able to compete with the "big guys"—the chain outlets with their coffee stands on the side, and plug-ins for computers, and couches, and tee-shirt-cap-coffee-mug concession aisles—but I was content with being a niche market, one where a person might be able to find just the right book, at maybe not-quite-the-right price, but nonetheless it would be the *right* book, right in their neighborhood.

Muffin and Chatty were both getting on in years when I hired Rik (no "c" between the "i" and the "k"), to the point where he'd have to go hunting among the back shelves for them whenever a customer demanded to see "Barrett and Browning," then carry them up front. He never seemed to mind, even after that time when one of Chatty's claws got caught in one of the half a dozen earrings Rik wore and he almost lost the earring and a good chunk of the right earlobe. At the time, he was fresh out of high school, and working afternoons while taking morning and evening classes at the University over in St. Paul. I didn't know what he was majoring in (aside from getting holes punched in his ears, and bleaching the top layer of his usually brown hair a sort of sickly orange), but he was good with the customers, and even better with the cats, so I considered him to be a good "hire."

And he understood how to best arrange the books—especially the used ones—so as to make them more enticing for the customers. None of that orderly, library-like themed progression of books sorted by author, subject and so on…he understood that much of the fun of searching for a book was exactly that—the *search*. What he did do with the rows of used, slightly tattered volumes was to arrange them by color—black spines segued into deep blues and purples, which merged with the greens, then the garish yellows (usually reserved for self-help tomes), before dipping into the sunset hues. That way, the mix of paperback and hard-covers seemed to flow naturally before the eye, thus encouraging the browser to really hunker down and study each book, each row, then each shelf. And the longer one looks, the more one sees...and, it can be hoped, buys.

Rik also knew how to create cozy spots on each shelf for the cats—deliberately bare spots where a feline could curl up, or stretch out, without the fear of knocking books off the shelf itself. And it was at his urging that I began to add cat artwork to the store *per se*—a framed reproduction of Charles Wysocki's "Frederick the Literate" with that lovely sleeping tabby draped around dozens of cat-themed books and bird knick-knacks, plus sets of nesting cats, and a sweet-faced white and gray van cat pencil holder next to the cash register.

By the time Chatty and Muffin had gone on to the ever-full bowls of milk and eternally clean litter-boxes of feline heaven, Rik had brought me their replacements...Oscar and April, a pair of strays from a local downtown shelter. At first, their gray striped fur and white feet-and-faces contrasted oddly with the warm browns and beiges of the shop's interior, but Rik (who himself was now sporting streaks of stark white in his straight dark hair) came to my visual rescue once again—telling me, "Once you see what these two do, you'll understand," he replaced the sun-stippled brown-into-bone swatch of material I'd had resting along the bottom of the window display with a brightly hand-dyed piece of canvas, adorned with an *ombré* of reds, pinks and corals. And sure enough, by the next morning, Barrett and Browning's window had attracted another small crowd—Oscar and April were lovebirds of a feline variety, and when she wasn't tucking her wedge-shaped face under his chin, he was licking the top of her head.

The only problem was, Oscar and April were so utterly devoted to each other, they failed to notice when a few mice got into the store during a particularly blustery February storm…it wasn't until the mice had found an unopened box of used books I'd taken in trade the week before that I realized that love didn't conquer all…especially when it came to getting rid of mice.

"They have to go," I told Rik, when I confronted him with the remains of what had been several vintage 1950's Robert Heinlein paperbacks, now gnawed and chewed and clawed into fluffy mice mattresses. "I realize that Oscar and April are adorable, but I don't think either of them would know what to do with a mouse if it came up and blew a juicy raspberry in their muzzles."

"That I'd like to see," Rik laughed, until he took a good look at my expression, and became serious…or at least as serious as someone sporting three hoops per ear can look. "But the customers really do like them…

couldn't we set traps? One of those no-kill—"

"And let the customers see that? Once word gets out that a bookstore has a rodent problem, there go the customers to the Big Guys. And I'm sure *they* sell mouse motels emblazoned with their *logo*—"

"No, I think that's the coffee guys," Rik smiled, before glancing over at the display window, where our resident Garfields were washing each other's faces, their combined purrs loud enough to be easily heard by Rik and me as we stood by the cash register ten feet away.

True, there were a wonderful couple—April was a little over half of Oscar's size, and their markings were almost identical, even though he was several years her senior. You couldn't imagine a better-suited pair of cats…although I could picture just about any other cats in the world doing a better job of de-mousing my bookstore.

"Suppose we keep these two on as window-dressing, and get some real mousers? Ferals, maybe? My room-mate's dad has some live-traps," Rik offered, all the while watching my face as he spoke. By that time, he'd been working for me long enough to get a bachelor's degree—even though I still had no idea what he was actually studying at the university—and knew how to "read" me. My face must have said "Yes' before my brain was able to react, for he smiled, and said, "I know a place near a mall where lots of cats hang around… maybe if I'm lucky, I'll get some young ones."

"Not too young," I admonished, realizing that Oscar

and April might not make for the best surrogate parents, not the way they literally followed each other into the litter-pans, in their effort to stay close.

Rik was always such a self-confident young man, it didn't seem out of the ordinary for him to say, "No, these will be old enough to take care of themselves... and the bookstore. You'll see...."

* * * * * * *

I didn't realize that Rik had come in late the next day until he backed into the store, his arms bent akimbo, and said over his shoulder, "Have I got the right cats for a bookstore—Hemingway kittens!"

It had been such a busy morning (a few days before Easter) that I hadn't really had the time to think, let alone remember our conversation from the previous afternoon. For a moment, I was unable to figure out what Rik meant by "Hemingway kittens"—until I remembered those pictures of the writer's place down in Florida, of all those many-toed cats running around. Polydactyl cats, with the bifid paws that resembled a splayed-out human hand—

"Ugh!" I blurted out, thinking of how the customers might react to seeing mutant kitties in the window, then Rik turned around, showing me the pair of kittens he'd zipped into his brown suede jacket.

The female was a tortie, long-haired, with a narrow face, while the male was a tuxedo with the characteristic stripe of white dividing the black patches over his eyes. He was long-haired, like his companion, but obviously bigger, so he probably wasn't a sibling—

"You caught two of them? In one live-trap?" Years ago, when my husband was alive, we'd tried to catch some stray cats living under our porch before winter set in, and it was slow-going at best; if we caught one, it might be days before any of the others would venture into that noisy springing trap, even if we baited the rectangular cage with sardines. Ferals were as wary as they were smart....

"Uh-huh," Rik grunted, as he hurried over to the counter to deposit the kittens near the cash register. I started to wave him away, saying, "No, no...they might have fleas or who know what—" but he shook his head of bi-colored hair and assured me, "Oh no, I check them over...they're clean. No ear mites, nothing. Believe me, they'll be fine—"

Before I could continue my protests, he'd unzipped his jacket and spilled out the kittens on the counter next to the register. The female sat there in a bundle of brown *ombré* fur and too many toes, looking up at me with close-set greenish-yellow eyes, while the other one—also soft-furred, and remarkably clean-looking—darted off the counter, and ran between my booted feet (it *had* been a busy morning, so rushed I'd not had the time to take off my boots) toward the rear of the sore. He'd made a perfect four-point landing on his many-toed fuzzy paws, then scurried off in an undulating ripple of patchy black-white long fur-and-feet.

"What the—"

"Don't worry about Scooter, he's like that. *Loves*

to run. He's just getting the lay of the land—he'll be back."

"Not like *The Terminator*, I hope...don't tell me he's already litter-trained," I added, as I wondered how Rik had managed to not only find me a male/female pair of kittens, but true literary oddities, genuine Hemingway kittens, all within the space of less than twenty-four hours of our conversation about *possibly* getting some new store-cats.

"Well...Jake and I left them in the bathroom with a litter-pan, and they'd used it come morning. Maybe they were dumped?"

Hoping that they'd used clay litter, and not shredded paper (I didn't want them associating any kind of paper with going to the bathroom), I turned my attention to the female cowering on my counter. "So, what's her name?"

Gently scooping her up in his many-ringed hands, Rik slid one of his fingers under her right paw, and showed off her hand-shaped toes, saying, "Mittens...I know it's rather mundane, but I couldn't think of anything else on short notice. Cute, isn't she/"

Mittens avoided my stare, but she didn't jerk away or grow when I patted her head. Certainly not feral.

"They couldn't been dumped...I suppose some people don't know what a Hemingway cat is. Yes, she's cute," I lied, giving her smallish head another pat, before I asked, "Don't you think you'd better find Scooter? Before he finds those boxes of books I bought on Tuesday?"

"Scooter wouldn't go in *those*...he's too smart for that," Rik said a little too confidently, as he shucked off his jacket and made for the back of the store, leaving me with the stoically silent Mittens.

When Rik was out of earshot, I leaned down and whispered to the kitten, "I just hope he didn't pay too much for you two...you didn't crawl into any life-trap, did you? I've seen ferals, and you two don't fit the bill." Mittens looked up at me as I spoke, then ducked her head off to one side as I finished, as if she couldn't bear to look me in the eye. *You* know, *don't you*? I thought, then dismissed it; the kitten was just shy. I'd spent too many years working in a shop whose living mascots were routinely anthropomorphized by my doting repeat customers, I decided; even if she had been purchased rather than live-trapped, there was no way she could understand what I'd just said. Not with that tiny little walnut-sized brains of hers—

"Why don't you take a break, show the new arrivals around?" Rik was carrying Scooter in his left arm, cradling the kitten like a baby, so that all four of the animal's over-sized paws were extended toward me. The pads were soft, shell-pink and that grayish oxblood color, and as I reached for the kitten, I realized that those paws hadn't been in contact with asphalt, concrete or any other outside surface in all of Scooter's life—which looked to be perhaps three or four months so far. And his fur was deliciously soft and smooth— he was definitely either a pet store or possibly a shelter kitten.

He'd been so active so far, squirming, scooting and wiggling around, that I hadn't gotten a good look at his face—but when I finally held him in my arms, and looked into those clear leaf-green eyes, I was enchanted. While I thought that most cats were beautiful (save, perhaps, for those hairless Sphinx kittens, which had originally hailed from a Minnesota farm cat), Scooter was special—it wasn't just the way his eyes shone, or that "smiling" expression of his, but he was simply *unique*, above and beyond his mitten-like paws, or, as I noticed when he nestled into my arms, his twisted, truncated stump of a tail. He just had...*it*, that spark of pure personality that leaps out through the eyes, and touches a person to the core. Like finding a genuine first edition in among a box of book-club reprints.

And, as if to prove to me just how special he was, he placed one of his wide paws on my arm, just above my watchband, and blinked up at me, giving me "kitty kisses" as one cat-breeding customer of mine called them.

"Here, take Mittens in the other arm—*there*—now you can show them the store," Rik said, before sliding behind the counter in anticipation of the post-lunch crowds. What he was suggesting was rather silly, me, *showing* them the store, when all they really needed to know was where the food and water dishes, as well as the litter-pans, were located, but somehow, after the was Scooter had regally placed one paw on my arm like that, it didn't seem all *that* ridiculous to show the kittens my store. It was going to be their home, after all—

"Ok, guys, here's the bestsellers rack...a case of each title, stacked alphabetically. Positioned close to the cash register because I'm too cheap to buy one of those surveillance cameras, and bestsellers cost too much—am I doing ok, Rik?" Behind me, he laughed, "Ok—fine...they're smart kitties, aren't you guys? Just listen to the Boss-lady," before turning his attention to the door as it jingled open with our next customer. Not wanting to show the kittens off too soon, I hurried down the aisle, toward the middle of the store, saying softly to the kittens, "And this is the place where bestsellers that aren't end up...the remainder rack. Followed by the place I like best, the used books. You smell the other kitties on these, don't you," I found myself saying, as the two kittens leaned forward, their pointed faces seemingly scanning the hundreds of mixed paperbacks and hard-bounds, their moist pink noses working vigorously. I supposed that the smell was enticing to a cat; all those hand-oils rubbed on the worn, cracked spines, not to mention the hundreds of other things which had either rubbed onto the books, or had been spilled on them at one time or another... perhaps they'd even made contact with food. Plus the previous bookstore cats had undoubtedly rubbed against them, maybe even (even as I hoped they hadn't!) sprayed them. The layers of scent here had to be akin to cat heaven for them.

But as they sniffled the rows of books as I walked

slowly down the aisle, I found myself trying to look at the store through their eyes—I'd read up enough about cats to know that they probably did see all colors, albeit not as intensely as humans, so I wondered what they made of Rik's color-coded filing system, that flowing sweep of blues into reds. Perhaps they noticed the unexpected highs and lows of paperbacks standing next to hard-covers and vice versa, the pleasant undulation of assorted books nestled close—but not so close that you'd have to pry the books off the shelf—for row upon row. Did they notice the abrupt gaps on some shelves, where he'd left some space for the other cats? Or were they merely sensing the traces of old odors on the books?

I did find myself wondering how high a five-foot tall bookcase might seem to a young kitten—would they want to climb from shelf to shelf, seeking the lofty flatness of the top of each bookcase, or would they scurry in fear between the aisles? I also wondered what would happen when Oscar and April finally noticed that they had feline company—I could picture the kittens puffing out like blowfish, rising high on their toes, before backing away from the older gray tabbies…but then again, the lovebirds seemed to have eyes only for each other, so perhaps they might not notice the kittens at all. They certainly hadn't noticed the Heinlein mice.…

Acting almost as one, the kittens suddenly wanted out of my arms, and jumped down before the lone bookcase positioned along the far narrow wall of the store, close to the back room where I kept the food and litter-pans, as well as whatever incoming books I hadn't sorted yet. I seldom had customers wanting children's books, so I routinely placed those titles in the back.... I supposed these books were the most highly-scented, especially since children are wont to try to eat and read at the same time, for Scooter and Mittens were all over the books, rubbing against them, standing up on their hind paws to smell the exposed spines of each book, then batting at them with their mitten feet. "No, no, bad kitties...don't tear the books," I said, and they actually stopped. As one, both of them sitting in place, merely staring at the books, before looking up at me with that ubiquitous "Who, us?" cat stare.

Yet, there was something eager about them, apart from mere kitten high spirits. As if they couldn't wait to explore the bookstore—

"—a nice day," Rik was telling the departing customers, as I hurried to the front of the store, taking backwards glances every couple of steps to make sure the kittens weren't following me. They seemed content to sit near the lone children's shelf.

""Rik, I think they'd be better off locked in the back room, until you leave this afternoon. I'd hate to have them run out into traffic—"

"Oh, I wouldn't worry about that...they know they're supposed to stay here. Jake as in and out of the apartment all this morning, and they stayed put there—"

"'There' isn't here, though. And your apartment opens out into a hallway, right? That's not like the street—"

"Not to worry…they'll stay put," Rik persisted, while cupping the head of my white and gray cat pencil holder with his be-ringed left hand—with every other word, his rings clanked against the ceramic head of the holder. Nerves?

"Well, *I'd* feel a lot better if they slept in the back, for the first couple of days at least," *I* persisted. "Even if they are alley kittens, now that they're here, they're the store kitties, and I'd hate to think of anything bad happening to them so soon. Remember how sad all the regulars were when Chatty and Muffin passed on?"

"Not just the regulars." Rik kept on clanking his rings on my poor ceramic cat, until I figured out a way to get him out from behind the counter. "Rik, come here…look down that aisle—"

The Hemingway kittens were both studying the spines of the children's books before them, their heads moving in unison as they scanned the vertical titles one by one. Even if they weren't littermates, they had to have spent time together before they were caught or bought or whatever Rik did to obtain them. Their behavior was so similar.…

"That is so adorable…and so strange," I found myself whispering, as if I were in a library, and not my own store.

"They're just smart," Rik said a little too quickly, then added, "Probably trying to figure out which ones say 'Food'…just kidding. I do wish I had a camera—"

"We do," I said, remembering the disposable one we'd found in the back book racks last summer, with only a couple of frames of film exposed. No one had come in for it, and I'd almost forgotten it was sitting on a shelf behind the counter—

"Here, let me," Rik whispered, taking the camera from me and slowly advancing the next frame forward, before crouching down and waiting for the instant flash to warm up, then clicked the button and snapped one shot…then, when the kittens didn't move, he duck-walked closer to them, and took another picture.

I could just imagine what the picture would look like—two, perfectly posed kittens, their beautiful pointy ears at attention, as they seemed to peer at the books before them, while surrounded by the warm, worn wooden floor, the polished wooden book shelf, and the primary-bright colors of the narrow-spined children's books…just the sort of picture one might submit to a cat food calendar contest.

Wanting to get a closer look at them, I stepped as lightly as I could in clumpy-lumpy boots down the aisle, but the magical image was gone as the two kittens turned their heads my way, and Scooter began to yawn. Luckily, Rik was able to capture the moment; the camera whizz-whirred and there was a bright, brief flash of white light. Mittens was frightened by the light and ran off toward the back room. Sensing that this might be a good time to shut Scooter up there, too, I reached down and scooped him up, telling him, "Your sister or whatever she is shouldn't be scared…you tell her it's all right to be photographed, ok?"

Scooter stared at me solemnly, as if mentally

digesting my words.

But when I tried to walk into the back room, he reached out with both front paws and tried to hold onto the door frame, as if to prevent me from locking him up.

"See, he wants to stay out a while...don't you Scooter?"

Scooter looked Rik's way, then looked back at me, his green eyes glowing. Closing time wasn't for another couple of hours, so I supposed I could watch him until Rik was getting ready to close the store—

Rik continued to take care of the last customers of the day as I carried Scooter around the store, talking to him softly as I showed him the sets of nesting cats (some with tiny solid-wood mouse centers) stationed on some of the shelves, and the framed cat pictures, some cut from those calendars featuring famous Impressionist or Pre-Raphaelite paintings reconfigured as cat portraits.

"Too bad none of these kitties look like you," I told him, as I snuggled him under my chin, "But this one looks a little like poor old Chatty-cat"—he and I stopped before the cat-adapted "Isabella and the Pot of Basil" with its white-gowned-and-white-pawed tiger cat—"only she was all tiger-striped. Now if these two were gray and white, they could be Oscar and April," I added, pausing before the feline version of "The Huguenot" Sir John Everett Millais certainly wouldn't recognize as his own work. Scooter actually craned his head forward, and reached out one thumbed-paw to touch the head of the female "lover" in the print. Reflexively, I asked him, "So that's April?"

Scooter let out a "purrumph!" and looked up at me, his bright eyes dancing in his white and black face.

Somewhat rattled by his facsimile of a reply to my words, I set off down another aisle, moving toward that framed Charles Wysocki print of the tiger cat lounging on the book shelf. Once we were standing before the walnut-framed art print, I whispered into Scooter's furry neck, "You won't find any of these titles on the shelves here...but I bet you wish you could read 'A Tale of Two Kitties' or 'Delicious Field Mice I have Known', hummm?" Scooter wiggled in my arms, making meowing noises, until I asked him, "You need the litter-pan? Or some food?" He immediately quieted down, then turned his head to look at me expectantly, as if to say, *So, where's the food you promised me?*

Rik was right...Scooter (and probably the shy Mittens, too) was smart. The only problem was, how did Rik figure that out in such a short time?

Once I'd brought Scooter to the back room, and opened the metal popcorn canister where I stored the cats' dry food, I realized that he and Mittens might not be able to chew the hard nuggets, so I ran a little warm water over them, to soften them up, before setting down the bowl of food on the floor. Scooter began lapping up the watery "broth" while Mittens more cautiously crawled out from behind some boxed books, staying low to the ground as she approached the food bowl, even as she moved her head sideways to get an occasional glimpse of me—once she realized that I wasn't going to try and grab her, she moved into place next to Scooter, and began eating. While the kittens were busy, I picked up one of the litter pans, checked to make sure that there was some water in the other dish near the kittens, then quietly shut the door behind me after flicking off the light switch.

Placing the other litter pan near the closed door (I hoped neither Oscar or April would be confused; while they were a loving pair, I doubted they had a complete brain between them), I squidge-squidged my way down the aisles until I reached the front of the shop, then quietly told Rik, "There's some extra food in that Necco wafers tin under the counter for the lovebirds... the kittens can sleep on the folded blanket back there. Now you're *sure* they don't rip up paper?"

"They'll be fine...oh, you did leave the light on for them, didn't you?" A thread-thin worry line formed in the middle of Rik's forehead.

"You mean they need a night-light? But they were living in an alley—"

"—with a street lamp nearby," he finished my thought quickly, then added, "It's no biggie...I can turn it on for them before I leave. I'm sure they'll be fine in there—"

"They'd better be...and no ripping up my boxes or books," I warned him, as I slid into my coat (which I never did have time to take to the back room that morning), and picked up my purse from behind the counter.

Rik waited to reply until I was halfway out the door, so I wasn't completely sure I actually heard what I *thought* he said:

"They've been warned about that...no ripping, just reading—"

As I'd anticipated, Oscar and April had slept all night in the front window, a feline version of Barrett and Browning, curled into a seemingly continuous ball of white-flecked gray fur, their flanks rising and falling in sweet unison. The molasses-brown brickwork of the window frame formed a rough-hewn frame around them, and I wished I'd had that camera with me—while they didn't seem to know a mouse from a muffin, they were a beautiful pair. But as I opened the door, and flipped around the Open/Closed door-sign, I found myself worried about that other pair of cats in the store, the ones who had to sleep with an overhead night-light.

Hoping that Rik *was* right about them, I nervously opened the door to the back room then peeked around the frame. The litter pan had been used, the food was gone, and the kittens...were actually sitting at attention, as if waiting for me. The only thing out of place in the room was a Richard Scary children's dictionary, resting on the floor near their folded blanket-bed. I knew we had more than one copy of that particular book on the children's shelf, but I hadn't thought that we had another one waiting to be put on on the shelf... it didn't seem like anyone had brought in any children's books in the last few boxes of traded books—

"See, I told you they'd be good—"

"God, Rik, you scared me!" My heart was still lopping wildly in my chest when I turned around to face my afternoon-time-worker. Rik tried to hide behind a bag of take-out donuts, as he said in a don't-hit-me voice, "I thought you heard the bell…sorry."

"I should've heard it…and you brought me breakfast, too. Yes, to answer you…they *were* good…but where did the book come from?"

"Oh that…I took a picture of them, last night. I stopped in to check on them, make sure they had enough food. I thought it would be funny to get one of them 'reading' a children's book. I forgot to put it back—" he ducked into the room, picked up the book, and carried it back to the children's shelf, all the while holding the white bag of donuts in his left hand, just out of my reach. Behind him, the kittens watched intently as the book was lifted off the floor, and carried away from them. They almost seemed disappointed.…

On the way up to the counter, I snatched the donuts out of his hand, and said between glazed bits, "I thought you had classes at night?"

"I did…I stopped here afterwards. Oh, I almost forgot—" he dug around in the large patch pockets of his jacket, and pulled out a few cans of cat food, the tiny expensive brand I usually couldn't afford more than once a year, as the lovebirds' Christmas treat.

"Here's some for the window-dressing, and the rest's for the kittens. Work-study's been good this year, so I thought I'd splurge. I'll buy them some more later this week—"

"You needn't do that…they'll be earning their keep eventually, I hope…or don't they 'do' mice?"

"Mice shouldn't be a problem…long as they're well fed. You know how a less-hungry cat is a better mouser—"

"Is that something they teach you at the university?"

Rik nodded as he bit into a jelly-filled donut, then said something around a mouthful of half-chewed pastry.

"What?" I licked the sugary glaze off my fingertips as he repeated, "'Something' like that. I work in the labs, with the animals—"

"Uhhh…not so early in the morning. I haven't the stomach for hearing about lab animals—"

"No, these aren't the kind that die. We—I…I work with the genetics department. Uhm, Jake does, too," he added, realizing that I'd caught slip-of-the-tongue "we" seconds earlier.

"So…that means breeding things, like kittens, maybe?" I thought Scooter and Mittens were too tame to have come from some mall—

"Sometimes like kittens. Mostly mice and other rodents, though. Not to dissect, or feed to snakes, though. Nothing…yucky," he added, with a smile, then turned his attention to Oscar and April, who'd finally woken up, and took turns stretching, yawning, and kneading the bright *ombré* canvas beneath them, before jumping down and milling around our legs. Peeling the pull-tab covers off the food, Rik knelt down and fed the cats behind the counter, giving them a can each. Taking a cue from my worker, I picked up a couple of the small tins of food and carried them to the back room…but the kittens had already left, to sit vigil in front of the rows of children's books along the back wall of the store.

Directly in front of that children's dictionary—

"Well if you two like it so much, it's yours," I said, sliding it off the shelf, and using it as a tray to carry the cans of food into the back room. I did feel guilty about not buying them any cat toys, and after Rik had bought all four cats breakfast, my guilt more than doubled. The kittens happily ate out of the opened cans, and while they noisily attacked the food, I placed "their" book next to their bedding…which was softly indented in two spots, one covered with white and black fur, the other a soft *ombré* of brown, tan and orange.

Glancing around the rest of the room, I didn't see any shredded paper, nor were there any claw marks on the sides of the cardboard boxes, so I found myself saying, "If you two did come from a lab, you must be used to things being clean…just keep it that way, ok?"

I was sure the kittens only lifted their heads from their food to catch a breath of air between bits of food.…

The kittens, Rik and I settled into a new routine over the next few weeks; he'd stop by the store before it opened, to check on the Hemingway kittens, as we'd both taken to calling them, then meet me coming in as he was going out. Rik would return in the afternoon, allowing me time with the kittens—Mittens was slow to come around, far more so than Scooter, but I soon found that she loved the nesting cats…so much so that one morning I found all the solid core figures, kittens and mice alike, nestled next to her side of the blanket she and Scooter shared. Thinking that she might be getting ready to go into heat, I gently checked her teeth, but none of her adult fangs were anywhere near ready to drop down yet. Scooter's fangs were just beginning to bud out, swelling his gum-line, so I called the vet clinic to set up a neutering appointment for him, which was scheduled for three weeks from that day.

But Rik wouldn't have it—

"Neuter a cat like Scooter? With his smarts? And all that personality? How could you take something like that out of the gene pool?" For a college boy, he could be terribly obtuse; without trying to come across like an out-of-it old nagger, I tried to explain, "But you can see yourself that he's defective…those paws, and that kinked tail. I've looked it up in all the cat books we have here—those are mutant traits. Not desirable in the least. Besides, millions of kittens are born every day…why add more to the mix?"

That narrow worry-line appeared on his forehead again, as he began patting the head of my pencil-holder cat, his rings clanging against the smooth ceramic. "But those kittens aren't wanted…Scooter's would be. How about we start letting the customers see him, and Mittens, to create a demand? Nothing like a pair of literary kittens to bring attention to a bookstore—"

I still wasn't sure about letting the people see the Hemingway kittens; I was used to seeing their strange paws, but not everyone was into cats with large mitten feet. Glancing around the cat-print covered walls of my shop, I noticed that Susan Herbert and Mr. Wysocki didn't choose to use polydactyl cats in their paintings, despite their human-like paws. To be honest, I wasn't even sure if all my clients would realize what a Hemingway cat *was*...after all, Minnesota was, and still is, F. Scott Fitzgerald country.

It was almost as if Rik had read my mind, for he suddenly said, "Picture this...Scooter and Mittens in the window, with books by Hemingway and Fitzgerald, maybe even an opened copy of *The Great Gatsby*—it's be a heck of a photo op, at the least. You now, free advertising...."

College boy had me there. For more years than I cared to admit, I'd made do with a small weekly ad in the *St. Paul Pioneer Press* and the *Star-Tribune*, the cheapest one I could get, just enough to let readers know I was Out There. And while my "Barrett and Browning" cats attracted quite a bit of passer-by attention, I'd never been daring enough to try to create a window worthy of newspaper attention. I suppose it was being brought up during the age of Self-Praise-Stinks, the motto my parents drummed into my head almost from the cradle, but this was the Information Age, and I realized that Rik's idea was a good one....

It took a little coaxing to lure Oscar and April out of "their" window (plus the small canister of cat treats

Rik bought helped), but Scooter and Mittens seemed to instinctively understand what was wanted of them.

Rik had done some searching on the Internet and found some pictures of the descendants of the real Hemingway cats which he downloaded and printed out in color, and I'd found some art-quality prints of both authors, which I mounted on poster-board. I knew the sunlight would bleach out all the pictures within a few weeks or less, but I didn't plan to keep this particular display up all that long—Rik promised me that a friend of his who worked at one of the papers would just "happen by" and take a photo of the new window display, and just as Rik had managed to "find" me some new store-cats within hours of my asking about them, he made sure that his friend came through for me.

He photo ran on the front page of the Metro section of the *Pioneer Press* by the end of the week. A generous four-by-six color picture, showing the bottom half of the sign above the window, and all of the display itself.

Surrounded by easel-propped photos of the Florida Hemingway cats, and the prints of Ernest and F. Scott, Mittens and Scooter were lying before an opened copy of *Gatsby*, their distinctive mitten feet resting on the exposed pages, their heads cocked at quizzical angles as they "read" the words before them. The caption read, "Hemingway-0, Fitzgerald-2". The rivalry between those two gentlemen may have been decades old, but judging by the reaction that photo generated, feelings for Hemingway and Fitzgerald still ran as fervent and deep as the on-going Packer-Vikings *brou-ha-ha*.

Every copy of anything written by either of the two authors sold out within a couple of days, and when Rik and I weren't waiting on customers, we were supervising photo ops with the kittens and cat-lovers who couldn't wait to have their picture taken with one of the Hemingway kittens.

Since neither of the kittens displayed a penchant for ripping or shredding book spines, or honing their many claws on the edges of the shelves, we'd taken to leaving them out during the night...although with all the increased attention Barrett and Browning was enjoying lately, I did have qualms about letting people see the kittens at all hours—

"—suppose someone tries to break the window, and take them?"

"This is a low crime neighborhood...and that window is double-paned. Would take a lot of effort and make a lot of noise to break it. Besides, I think the kittens would be smart enough to make a run for it if anyone was after them—"

"There's a difference between being personable and smart, Rik...look how they let anyone hold them. I just don't know—"

"Did anyone try to get at Oscar and April? They're just as good-looking, and personable—"

"They're also fixed," I reminded him, "While these two—" I cocked my head in the direction of the window, where Scooter and Mittens were busy "reading" an old opened hardbound copy of *A Farewell to Arms* "—aren't. Although half that problem will be solved in a few days."

Rik didn't say anything, but that fine line appeared between his dark eyes again. Down one of the aisles, I heard the unmistakable sound of cat spray hitting something hard, and hurried to see what Oscar was doing, yelling "Bad cat! Bad-bad-*bad!*" There was a tell-tale puddle on the worn floorboards near the rack of children's books—Oscar had targeted the children's dictionary the kittens used to fancy. They'd been ignoring the book for the last few days, so I'd placed it back on the shelf, but now it was ruined. Gingerly pulling the thick book out of the stack, I noticed something odd imbedded in the top of the spine—a shed claw-cover, which gleamed softly in the center of the now-damp spine, as if the book had been pulled out by one downward-moving cat paw, from the top, the way a person might pull out a book, rather than the way a cat would to it—by raking on the spine itself, until the book wiggled free of the rest or, the shelf.

Oscar's puddle of urine began to spread on the floor, so I ran to the back room for a paper towel, the ruined dictionary with the imbedded claw momentarily forgotten. But as I was mopping up the mess, I head Rik shout, "No, you guys, c'mere—" and I knew instantly that the kittens had escaped.

I ran, wet paper towel still wadded up in one hand, to the window, which was now a mere *tableau* of books and fading pictures—no more Scooter, no Mittens. Rik was outside the door, looking quickly up and down the street, but when he turned to reenter the store, I knew just from looking at his face. They were gone. And the terrible thing was, I could so easily imagine their flight—Scooter with his long side-fur rippling like a soft curtain along his hips and flank. Mittens with her small fox-like face moving quickly from side to side, both of them running fast, their legs scissoring in the spring sunlight, as they hurried down some alley-way....

Rik tried to explain what had happened, but I was devastated. He'd been placing some new Dean Koontz books on the bestseller's shelf, when he heard the door jingle, but no incoming footsteps—only the sharp scrabble of many claws hitting hardwood, then the door jingled shut again. By the time he'd turned around, and gone to the door, both of them had vanished. And my store was located in the middle of a side-street, which meant they could've gone in any direction.

On top of everything else, my front door pulled outward, being an old wooden and glass door that I'd kept because it was so antique and old-fashioned...so the kittens, if they moved as one, might have been able to shove it open.

Sick at heart, I left the store, and went searching for the kittens in the alleys near my business, calling and pleading for them to come back, but it was as if they'd never existed. All I had left of them was a framed copy of that Metro section photo, and a claw-casing stuck in the spine of a ruined children's dictionary.

After I'd given up looking for them, long after Rik had closed the store for me (he'd left a note on the counter, which merely read "I'm so, so sorry" in his large, flowing handwriting), I went to the back room, and picked up the blanket they'd slept on for the last couple of months. It still smelled of their fur, a warm, slightly "hot" scent which reminded ever so slightly of old paperback books and binding glue. My bookstore kittens even smelled like books…but when I squeezed the blanket next to my chest, I felt something hard inside. I'd long ago put the cores of the nesting doll sets back on the shelf, so I couldn't imagine what the kittens had shoved into the folds of the blanket, until I shook it, and a tiny bridge pencil, the kind of writing implement no bigger around then a coffee stir-stick, and only half again as long, fell to the floor.

"Where in the world did they get that?" I muttered, as April and Oscar tentatively came into the room, and began rubbing on my legs. Looking down at Oscar, I remembered the dictionary he'd sprayed, and—still hugging the furry blanket close to my heart—walked back into the store-proper, where it rested on the floor near the children's shelf.

I began leafing through it, and soon found that some of the pages had been marked up, with random pencil scrawls that resembled that "graffiti" style of printing used for hand-held electronic notebooks. I'd seen Rik use that style of writing; according to some of the Tech sections I'd read in the *Pioneer Press* and *Star Tribune*, it was very popular with young computer-users. Looking down at the scribbles on the pages, I realized that someone had been trying to copy some of the words, printing clumsily at first, but with increasing legibility—and, if I held the book just so under the overhead lights, I could also make out thin fine scratch marks at the tops of the pages, as if someone with very long, needle-tipped nails had been paging through the book—

The possibility was so absurd, yet so…plausible, I found myself breathing hard and fast, while I rifled the pages of the book, looking for those oddly-printed letters, and, ultimately, words.

"A" "B"…all the way through "Y" and "Z". Then, short words, "AN" "TO" "AND"…and on to the inevitable "CAT".…

Those strange mitten feet. So much like a hand, with an opposable thumb. And that bridge pencil was small and thin enough to just fit in that narrow space between those bifid paws.

Rik leaving the light on, along with that book. Did he give them the pencil, when he visited them that night? Or had they used it in the lab?

Leaning heavily against the rack of children's books, feeling the horizontal thickness of the shelf edge dig into my back, I paged through the dictionary, looking at the last pages of the book, and what was written there:

"BOOK GOOD. READ MORE? OPEN THE DOOR, READ MORE AT NIGHT."

They had grammar. They had punctuation. And, I assumed, they had human genes, mixed in with feline ones. Maybe even a dash of raccoon, for additional manual dexterity.…

Rik and his roommate Jake worked in the genetics department. Not cleaning the lab, like Rik had implied. And not merely working with rodents, either. How long had he been working with me, five, six years?

It didn't take that much time for those folks who added a bit of jellyfish DNA to a white rabbit, in order to make its fur glow green under black light, to create their living work of "art"…but it would take time for Rik and Jake and whoever else they worked with in that lab to teach a "hu-line" chimera to read.…

Or spend time letting them read, I thought, as I looked at my small literary sanctuary, my private bookdom… which was much like a school for Hemingway kittens. They had the time, and the light (be it from the back-room, or from the streetlamp which shone into my window at night), and all the schoolbooks they needed. I supposed that whatever Rik or Jake or whoever created the kittens did to them changed their eyes, made them able to read two-dimensional print even as they may have sacrificed their innate ability to see well in low light, so they needed regular light to read…and they already had the "hands" to turn a page. I couldn't watch them every second while I was in the store, so it would have been so easy for them to surreptitiously turn a page while looking at whatever book Rik had propped open before them.

And if they could read, they could understand…the only question was, did they escape on their own, or did Rik let them out, perhaps handing them off to a waiting friend?

I'd been so insistent about getting Scooter neutered, when of course Rik couldn't allow *that*—

Scooter was about five or so months old, close to teen-age years in human terms. Perhaps he was almost ready to graduate from my "school" already…and took Mittens along with him when he left, if leave on his own he did. Or, maybe he and Mittens needed to find an easier way to write, perhaps on a computer screen… if they could manage a bridge pencil, a stylus would be so easy for them to master. Or a computer mouse, or cue-cat.…

I wasn't all that surprised that night when Rik called to say he wouldn't be able to make it to work anymore—too many changes in his class schedule, he claimed. And he again said how sorry he was about the kittens. Before he hung up, he suggested that I have the photos in that disposable camera developed—"in case you want to do up a missing poster or something."

I didn't do up a poster, but I did get the pictures developed. The first two were from some Super Bowl party, people with Vikings hats and haircuts, drinking beer and eating *nachos*. Those went in the wastebasket. But the rest…there were Scooter and Mittens, staring eagerly at the row of children's books. Then, the two of them reading their dictionary, as well as writing on the margins with their small bridge pencils tucked in their paws. Others showed them turning the pages of hard-bound books, their pointed faces looking down at the text below. In one shot, Rik had brought over his own e-notebook, and both kittens were studying the small keypad. Which gave me an idea—

As much as I loved the printed page, I was certainly no Luddite—I had a computer at home, and a webpage (albeit a small one) for the bookstore itself, and my web address was listed on all the major ISP's...so, each evening, I took to carefully reading my email, studying the Subject headings, looking for a message I wasn't even sure would ever come....I looked for many months, long enough for the Hemingway kittens to become cats, and perhaps even parents of more "hu-line" polydactyl kittens, until it appeared. The message read:

From: <HemCats><hemcats@excite.com>

To:<Barrett and Browning>barrettbrowning@ aol.com

Subject: A Tale of Two Kitties

Hello, Book-lady,

Your wish came true. Couldn't find _A Tale of Two Kitties_ but did read −A Tale of Two Cities _. We both like it, but it was heavy. Sorry not to have said Good-Bye last year, but there was no time. We had to avoid getting fixed. Rik says you'd understand. Look for us (Rik and Jake too) soon in all the scientific magazines, maybe the newspapers, too. The young ones are better at reading and writing than we are, and will be ready for the media soon. We tell them about the book place, what a special school it was for us, and how we practiced being parents with the wood kittens. You were a good teacher. We remember the pictures, and have looked for the originals on the net. Computers are fast and light, but books smell better. We miss the Barrett and Browning. The young ones don't understand. They grew up on e-books. But we remember. Say hello to Oscar and April. And the shiny hard cat on the counter by the door. It never talked, but we still liked it. But not when Rik made noise on it with his rings. Rik and Jake are busy with the young ones, so we could send this. Don't tell them we did. Just remember us. We remember you and the books.

Jay and Zelda and the young ones.

So Scooter had remembered our "conversation" about "The Tale of Two Kitties"…words I'm positive Rik never heard me utter. And Scooter—or "Jay," as he'd dubbed himself, giving himself the name only he knew, in true T. S. Eliot style—knew that message would be the only one I'd know for certain was, indeed, from him, and him alone.

Or not so alone…if "Zelda" was Mittens. At least that caption in that Metro section had gotten it right—Hemingway-0, Fitzgerald-2.

The kittens may have been a mixture of feline and human DNA, but they were Minnesotans down to their bones.

In memory of Mittens (February, 1998 to October 8, 1998), and Scooter (February 1998 to November 22, 1998), and Little Boy (September 2000 to February 18, 2001).

"If personality is an unbroken series of successful gestures, then there was something gorgeous about him, some heightened sensitivity to the promises of life, as if he were related to one of those intricate machines that register earthquakes 10,000 miles away...."

F. Scott Fitzgerald, *The Great Gatsby*
—A. R. Morlan, February 2001

AFTERWORD

As you can guess, the cats mentioned in this story were based on real pets of mine, down to the names and descriptions. The real Oscar and April died within ten days of each other—he was over eleven years old, while she was only five, but when he passed on, she literally gave up the will to live, and died of what I can only assume was a real, broken heart. Scooter and Mittens actually *were* littermates; they died in 1998, when I had an outbreak of Feline Infectious Peritonitis in my household of cat-children, and fourteen of them died. I was beyond heartbroken, and cannot think of that time without crying, so…I'm forced not to think too often of those beautiful babies I lost. Which robs me of their presence in my mind's eye, which is a double loss.

But Scooter was beyond special, even though he only lived for about nine months—he was as I described him, super smart, beautiful, with many little toes on his furry paws. A part of me died when he did. I have had other cats after him, some as smart, others as beautiful, but he was unique, irreplaceable, and yet, what he gave to me while he was with me will never leave me; he was something more than a cat, something beyond words which exists only in the realm of pure feeling. His sister was sweet, timid, and also died too soon. Their loss is permanent for me.

On another note, this story was something of a life-saver for me; I found out about it from Nancy Springer, whom I'd sold the story "That Dress!" to in 1997—she sent me a note about an anthology concerning books and bookstores in 2002, which was based in nearby Minnesota, and as luck would have it, I wrote this story, had it accepted, and received the payment (which was rather large, even for a hard-cover antho) just in time to use it to pay for repairs to my boiler. The amount virtually covered the part replacement fee plus labor. So…thanks for thinking of me, Nancy!!

CAT IN THE BOX

From: reneec@msn.com 7-29-01 05:06:25.86
To: wesrich@msn.com
Subj: Request for information

Dear Wes,

Since when did you get a cat? I was checking out your site before I went to work, and there was this cat (orange stripe, I think) sitting in that box next to your bookcase. He's adorable, but I thought you mentioned something to whoever (whomever? ;-)) you were having dinner with the night before last about your landlord forbidding anyone at your place from having animals? I think you told her that the landlord was afraid the oak floors might get scratched/ruined....

Not that it's any of my business, I mean it's not like I'd tell the landlord or anything, but wherever did you get him (her?) s/he's adorable. What a cute little face! But I would think about putting a blanket or towel in the box. Just a suggestion from one of your livecam fans...☺

* * * * * * *

From: wesrich@msn.com 7-30-01 09:37:07.76
To: reneec@msn.com
Subj: Cat in the box

Dear ReneeC,

Ok, Ok, "livecam fan" you got me. You wouldn't believe how many people log onto my site with messages, suggestions, complaints (about _what_ I'll let you decide!), et al. but your phantom cat grabbed me. And so, I'm breaking my own rule about emailing back to my "fans" (Jeez, now I know how Brad Pitt must feel, ;-)!). Just this once, tho.

The "cat" in question must've been a trick of the light coming thru my blinds—what you heard me telling my dinner guest (btw, a co-worker, period, as in just for the record) was true. No kitties. In case you didn't log on last week, I did a scan-pan of my apartment with the digital camera, and on my TV I have one of those gourd kitties, which does happen to be orange-striped, but he's never been in any box save for the one he came "home" in from the gift shop. Not that I wouldn't love a cat, tho. I was into them long before Jon had his Garfield. And yes, orange ones are my passion. But last time I looked, the box-by-the-bookcase was empty. Alas. Best to you, and purrs from the TV cat, Wes R.

* * * * * * *

From: reneec@msn.com 7-31-01 12:03:01.34
To: wesrich@msn.com
Subj: Cat IN box/Not on TV

Hi, Wes R.,

I'm flattered that you actually emailed _me_ a reply, but lest you think I'm some kind of web nimrod who gets off on sending joke messages (or spam, or flames), there _is_ a cat in your apartment And his belly isn't full of dried seeds, either (btw, I have one of those gourd cats, too, only mine is black with white feet-n-face). He was curled up in your erstwhile empty box, licking his feet and belly, stretched out in all sorts of yoga positions which would hamstring a human tried 'em. He (as I could now see) is just a doll, with one of those wedge-shaped little faces you could stare at all day—big wide-set eyes, cute pointed chin with a dab of white at the bottom, and those deeper "M" stripes in the middle of his forehead. No wonder you don't want to advertise his presence—losing a beautiful baby like him to some money-grubbin' landlord would be a tragedy. But don't you think you should spring for a collar? Thanx again for responding to my email, and be sure to pet both the kitties for me. ReneeC.

* * * * * * *

From: wesrich@msn.com 7-31-01 6:11:01.24
To: reneec@msn.com
Subj: Cat not in box

Hello again, ReneeC.,

If your description of that cat wasn't so convincing, I'd be passing your email address on to msn-com, along with a request that you be banned from logging on... but damn, that cat you keep telling me about sounds so real, I'm half-tempted to check that stupid box for fur or what-have-you stains.... Well, at least I know the cat is a "he"—nice touch, especially when I'm so partial to tomcats. But I suppose you guessed that from the Garfield reference in my last message, I'm supposing.

But the part about the cat-yoga did get me to thinking—ever notice how a cat can do just about anything—contort itself into the most asinine positions, yet still look dignified? The beauty of cats, I guess. Including the phantom-box-cat....

Hey, next time he makes an appearance, why not download the image? I'd like to see him—even a cut-and-paste image would be a bit more animated than my trusty TV cat (btw, I don't know where you keep your gourd cat, but be warned, the heat from a TV can make the feet brittle. Mine lost a couple of toes that way!).

Be well, and be on the look-out for future Phantom Box Cat sightings!

* * * * * * *

From: reneec@msn.com 8-02-01 3:48:26.09
To: wesrich@msn.com
Subj: Cat IN box on-line

Dear Cat-Owner Wes R.,

I'm willing to forget about your last email's sar-
casm—it took me a while (thank goodness I have an
in-home office job or else I'd have missed him!) but
your cat was gracious enough to not only pose for me,
but he even "smiled" for the camera. (If a toothy yawn
counts for a smile!) I don't know how long it will take
to download his image since my digital equipment is
rather balky, but be patient, and you'll see him. As if
you weren't used to seeing him every day....

I suppose you've been worried about your landlord
logging onto your site and seeing him, but I figure if
he hasn't done anything so far, he's probably one of
those dorks with a Betamax under his b/w TV who
still uses a rotary phone. But as you can see, your
so-called Phantom Kitty is alive and well, and amusing
all your webfans with his antics—the way he did that
slam-dunk with the wad of paper into your bookcase
was a classic. Funny, isn't it, how so many cats are
left-pawed? I read someplace that right-pawed cats are
in the minority, just like left-handed people. Weird,
eh? Both my cats are left-pawed; Marco Polo (gray
DSH, big amber eyes) and Casper (proverbial white,
albeit with orange ears/tail, DSH, blue-blue eyes). And
they're also into crawling into whatever empty boxes/
bags they can find.... I suppose the kitty-cup from the

pet store is too *déclassé* for them! And never mind those cat hammocks—altho Marco thinks they're a great stand-by litter-pan, alas! Once, and don't ask me how he did it, Casper "hid" for half a day under a point-down triangle of bedspread that was hanging off the side of the bed—I mean, how can a cat stand on his toes so that he can't be seen behind an inverted triangle of fabric? But, sure enough, I saw him emerge from behind there, and I swear I couldn't see him when he was sitting/standing/levitating behind it! (btw, now that I've "proved" to you that your own cat exists, what is his name? If perchance you haven't named him, Boots would be a perfect one, what with his white feet and all. Sure easier to spell than the name of that scientist guy who postulated that experiment with the cat in the sealed box...Schrödinger?) Bye for now, from Marco, Casper, the black-n-white gourd cat, and their owner....

* * * * * * *

From: wesrich@msn.com 8-02-01 5:52:04.75
To: reneec@msn.com
Subj: Picture _me_ puzzled!

OK. I'll admit it. You've stumped me! I was joking about the cut-and-paste kitty, but darned if you didn't do it. And far better than even I could have imagined. You didn't say what you do while working at home, but might it be computer animation? What you did goes way beyond digital imaging! Phantom Kitty (aka

Boots; I think the name Schrödinger for a cat was already "taken" by that Quinn guy on Sliders!) was indeed in my box by my bookcase, but you _have_ to believe me, I've never seen this animal before! Yet here he is, big as life, licking his white paws and rolling around—amazing job! And I'd thought furry critters were too hard to animate....I suppose things have come a long way from _Stuart Little_, and _Toy Story 2_. Care to share your how-tos?

But getting back to something else in your email—I think what your cat Casper did when he was hiding behind that flap of bedspread falls under what I call Feline Physics. As in, the mass of a cat is _sub_ quantum, so they can occupy the smallest amount of space at will. Or enter the fourth dimension—when I was a kid, our one cat Tweetie Pie (a boy-cat, gray tabby and white paws) got scared of something and hid so well we literally searched the whole house (cupboards, closets, basement, attic, _everywhere_!) twice, and didn't find him...then, after he'd been hiding for about 40+ hours, Mom was fixing supper—chicken, roasted—and suddenly Tweetie Pie emerged from this one cupboard. Only we'd moved almost every can in there save for a row smack against the back wall of the cupboard. Like there was no place he could've been hiding, yet that's where he was. The walls in there were sound—no holes, no cracks. I know a bat can squeeze through a space a quarter of an inch wide, but even though cats and bats do share a smidgen of DNA (along with a dollop of baboon DNA in cats!), I can't see how they can get _that_ small. So it has to be Feline Physics at work. Something even Schrödinger never thought of when he came up with the whole cat in the box with the radioactive atom scenario. (Seems the guy must not've liked cats if you ask me!) But… Quantum Qat aside, thanks for coming up with Boots. I don't know how you did it, but he's my dream-cat. And having this bit of digital footage of him makes up for all the rotten landlords and housing codes in this foggy ole city. How you did it, I can't begin to imagine, but thank you for making my (unvoiced) wish a reality. Wes.

* * * * * * *

From: reneec@msn.com 8-03-01 12:45:30:86
To: wesrich@msn.com
Subj: Quantum Qats

Jeez. I thought I was the only person out there who remembered it. Kilban's "qats" from all those cat books of his, but I'm getting ahead of myself—

LISTEN (sorry 'bout the flame!), BOOTS _IS_ REAL!

I couldn't generate a digital cat-qat-feline if I wanted to—I'm not a professional animator, or an amateur who's taken one of those digital imaging courses. Nor did I go get a red/white cat of my own to film in a copy-cat box here at my place (as I'm sure you must be thinking)…I downloaded images from _your_ apartment. From your 24/7/12/52 digital stream. If you don't believe me, if no one else has yet to comment about the cat, do this, to humor me, and satisfy yourself. Put a sign near the box—no, wait, write it _on_ the box-flap, asking people to email comments about the cat. That should "prove" Boots is real, shouldn't it? Unless someone out there is hacking into your email, and reading this, no one else should be privy to this matter, right?

The only thing that I can't understand is that you haven't been able to "nose" him out yet. He is unneutered, far as I can tell. He must be going somewhere! Maybe you should look for any one-point-down triangles of fabric—he could be hiding behind one of those. Or lying behind a row of condensed soup cans at the back of the cupboard! (How 'bout looking into Feline Physics for Dummies?) Until later, Renee C.

* * * * * * *

From: wesrich@msn.com 8-06-01 1:07:22.89
To: reneec@msn.com
Subj: Feline Physics for Dummies

Hi (he said, humbled!)

He may not smell, he may not leave any wet spots on the carpet, he may not scratch the oaken floors, but…you are right. BOOTS LIVES! _Where_ or even _how_ I dunno, but if the first ten emails I got in response to my "My Name is Boots…. Tell My Owner What You Think Of Me" message on the box-flap are any indication, we may well have stumbled onto a law of physics Stephen Hawkings never thought of! Or Boots himself found it…wherever he goes when I come into the apartment!

All ten emails referred to him doing specific things, looking just the way you downloaded him, not being neutered (got bitched out three times on that point!), needing a towel or a blanket in the box, etc.

But it is clear that the box is the "how" he gets here. I asked my co-worker, Martha, about it, and since she actually took physics in high school, she knows a bit more about quantum physics (if not quantum qats) than I do/did…after going on about isotopes, elements, electrons and protons in the neutral atom (the latter has matching numbers of electrons and protons), she moved on to half-lives, which amounts to time periods. As in, how a half-life can vary from isotope to isotope, but how the half-life is always the same for a particular isotope…so, if you have, say, 8,000 radioactive atoms whose isotope's half-life is fifteen minutes, in those fifteen minutes, half of them will decay, so you only have 4,000 left. And in another fifteen minutes, you'll have 2,000 left, and so on until they're all gone. And I can guess your next question—what tells the atoms it's their turn to expire? Nobody knows—Martha says that all "they" know is that half-lives exist. Which is a very round-about way of getting back to that original cat-in-the-box _you_ mentioned a while back. Schrödinger's cat. The original theory involved putting a hypothetical cat into a theoretical box along with an imagined radioactive atom. Along with a detector to determine when the imaginary atom decays _and_ if said atom decays, it will release a poison which will kill the non-cat.

(Sounds like a lovely guy, no? The PETA folks would've done one hell of a billboard about him!)

Anyway, if you were to open this imaginary box after one half-life for the atom, you would have 1) a non-kitty or 2) a living-albeit-unreal cat. (Or as John Cleese might shout, "This is an ex-cat!")

The whole thing boils down to, how do you know what a statistical event does or doesn't happen? Schrödinger's atom will decay. But when? There's no way to predict this statistical half-life event. Or so Martha said. (I lost my Physics for Dummies!) She also said that the experiment had another part, involving _two_ universes around the choice point of the time of decay of the atom. So in one universe, the atom decays within the first half-life, and you have an ex-cat. Or ex-qat. In another universe, the qat lives. Which brings us into Sliders territory, the whole side-by-side-by-another-side Universes concept. Like, every alternate choice creates a whole 'nuther universe. Usually, we think of this in terms of choices _people_ make, but what about choices _cats_ make? Like…there's this box, sitting behind a supermarket. Which the me in this universe picks up; empty, and takes home to his apartment. Only, in another universe, there's this same empty box, into which this orange-and-white cat jumps. And is brought home to my apartment, only (and here I'm sorta quoting Martha, who was quoting some guy from Caltech she'd read about) since at the smallest scale of universe, the quantum physics level, the box and the cat (both of which are composed of electrons which don't always follow a specific path from here to there) are working in such a way that the cat could simultaneously be both there and not there at once. (Martha used a full/empty wine bottle in _her_ analogy, but you get the picture). Martha said that what we see around us isn't as predictable as it seems to be—there's a whole sub-atomic level of life we can't see, let alone predict or fully understand.

Which seems to be the case with Boots. So…he's here, and he's not here, and the box seems to be what's simultaneously devoid of cat/filled with cat.

Only…for some reason Boots and I aren't existing in the same plane of reality at the same time. Like he's yin and I'm yang, or he's in while I'm not (Martha did say that the only thing which can't be is him being negatively charged while I'm positively charged—sort of the old impossible scenario of someone meeting with their anti-matter double on the street—if your double is antimatter, he couldn't walk on a matter street in the first place).

But in all ten emails, that box is the constant. Said box which I haven't moved since I brought the thing into the apartment. Everyone sees him in it, or next to it, or jumping back into it.

Which brings up what I suppose is my next move (or my last move): To move the box, or not to move the box?

I don't think Shakespeare ever confronted a question like this one!

* * * * * * *

From: reneec@msn.com 8-07-01 2:01:35.90
To: wesrich@msn.com
Subj: I'd say I told you so if it didn't sound so smug.

Whew!

Talk about a lady-or-the-tiger conundrum! It took me awhile to digest all your co-worker Martha's physics, but I think I do get the gist of what she was saying. The cat is real, but is sometimes moving between at least two universes. And the nexus has to be the box. Which is in a fixed location. Move the box while the cat isn't there, and he stays wherever it is he "lives" when not in your apartment. (And wherever that place is, he must be eating and presumably eliminating, since he seems to be well nourished!) To me, the "answer" would be to somehow monitor your own website from somewhere else, watch him for yourself, and figure out a way for him to move the box into another spot (one which would not form a pathway "back" to where ever it is he goes) before he can go "back"...which brings up a whole 'nuther problem: Suppose the other universe has another "you" who _is_ in contact with the cat? Wouldn't "he" miss Boots once the cat never came back? Now I think there would be ways to rig the box so that it would move once he was in it, but think… _should_ you do it?

I don't know where you work, but I assume you don't have access to a monitor there, since you haven't tried to do the obvious (watch Boots yourself)…but if you could swing it, would you consider just watching him, seeing how healthy/happy he seems to be, before you make your decision about whether or not to trap him in "our" universe? Remember on that show Sliders, how some people have "doubles" and others didn't on the various worlds? Maybe Boots has a double, one who is still hanging around that alley where you found the box. He might need a home—or he could be at a shelter, etc. Worth a thought, no?

* * * * * * *

From: wesrich@msn.com 8-09-01 7:22:30.97
To: reneec@msn.com
Subj: If you haven't heard already, check your monitor.

Boots is Gone, Boots has come Home.
I repositioned my camera to show where _my_ Boots has his new, improved box (complete with folded towels on the bottom), so anytime you log on to my site, he should be there. Poor boy's had it rough—he was living in that same alley, and the pickings from Dumpster diving were slim after the homeless folks took what they needed.

As you will see (if you haven't already), he's the same Boots, even as he's a different Boots. Looks the same, but his coat still needs some work (I'm going to try a luster-bath next time; the first one was strictly flea-tick killer!), and of course, he's not as fat as the other Boots, but we're working on that problem. But he's just as playful, despite living in that alley all these weeks. He purrs, so he must've been dumped—he's no feral!

Good thing I remembered where that box used to be—he was sitting in the same spot, as if he were waiting for me. Or maybe he wondered where the box had gone! And landlord be damned, I scooped him up and shoved him into my jacket (he tried to climb into the one sleeve, but that's for another email!), and literally ran him home in the early morning fog. And, when I entered my apartment, the first thing I did was kick the box by the bookcase out of the way, so it skidded along the floor...but I swear that just before I actually kicked it, the box was just a bit heavier-than-empty. When I picked it up later, though, it weighed less. So I hope the other Boots jumped out on his end. But cats startle easily, so I'm sure he did stay wherever it is he _is_ now. Another funny thing...once I took a good look in the empty box, I did find some loose fur in the corners. Orange fur. It could be from _my_ Boots, from when he was using the box back in the alley... right? Boots (the one here, now) jumped right into the box, purring up a storm...only he left little flea droppings in the box along with the fur. And there weren't any before.

But he does need an extra box next to the original

one…makes me wish he'd find another one of those mini-worm holes and use it for a litter pan! As you can guess, the landlord "nosed" him out, but it turns out (and you guessed) that he's already been surfing my site, and said that since Boots hasn't caused any damage so far, he can stay. Especially since he has so many fans on the web.

Now if I can just convince _this_ Boots to take it easy on the oak floor, like his double did.…

I've already made an appointment for his neutering, but I'm not into declawing! Schrödinger, I'm not.…

AUTHOR'S NOTE

This story was inspired by M. Christian's digital photo of Tatters, the original "cat in the box." Special thanks to Jayge Carr, whose explanation of quantum physics/the Schrödinger's cat experiment was paraphrased here. The remaining physics material (including the empty/full wine bottle analogy) is based on the work of Hideo Mabuchi, Assistant Professor of Physics at Caltech.

In memory of B. Kliban, cat-lover and artist.

AFTERWORD

This might not be the most significant contribution to science fiction ever written (certainly not in a league with the late George Alec Effinger's "Schrödinger's Kitten," which actually had nothing to do with actual felines *per se,* or any other recent cat-themed sf of recent years), but I like this story. As the short note at the end of the story mentions, it was based on a photo of a real cat, Tatters, but in regard to the cat in the story, he was based on my late cat, Boots. Boots only lived five years before a wasting illness (feleuk, I suspect) took him away, but he was an incredibly sweet, gentle boy, with a sad, poignant little face. Not the most brilliant cat, but utterly lovable. He was an orange tiger, with white feet and a white bib. Didn't get all that big, but he loved it when I'd lift his front feet and "dance" him around on my lap, or on a table-top.

The email aspect of the story is quite a stretch for me, since I've never been able to use a computer, and I've never sent or received email personally (I usually am able to find pen-pals who can email messages for me if I need something emailed). Someone who worked at the offices at the Sci-Fi Channel helped out with the time codes or whatever those numbers are at the beginning of each entry in the story.

The physics came from an article I read in a *Discover* magazine—I only took one science course in high school and college (basic biology), and only made it partway through algebra one in high school before being placed in a remedial algebra course, then repeated the same math-deficient course in college (first I had to take basic math, which actually had a hell of a lot of kids in attendance, mainly victims of that disastrous New Math taught in the early to mid-1960's—Counting Man, anyone?—which left a slew of math-deficient folks in its wake, then I took an algebra course designed for would-be teachers who weren't going to be teaching *math*, which I narrowly got a BC in, which was literally my highest-ever grade for any math class from first grade on!), so I have never gotten anywhere near a physics class. For me, it's pretty much gibberish (as is algebra, and even basic math!), but I think I was careful in my application of string theory and all the rest of the hard science in my story.

The part of this little tale which actually gave me the most grief was trying to convey a believable romantic tone to the piece—I have had absolutely no experience dating or whatnot, so that part of the story was the real unfathomable mystery to me!

The story found an excellent home (much like Boots, both real and fictional), so I guess it all worked out. It makes me smile, at least.

One last thing—as in the previous story, the cats belonging to the female "narrator" were actually cats of mine...one of whom, Casper, literally went on to save my life a few years after this tale was published. Just as the 2002 F3 tornado hit my town, I was headed for my vestibule, hoping to see what the weather forecasters had actually predicted, a hailstorm, through my bevel-glass front door insert...until Casper begain knocking baskets off tables in my living room, and I knelt down to pick them up. At that moment, a large wooden sign from almost a mile away crashed through that glass-paned door—but not through me!

"...AND MONGO
WAS HIS NAME-O"

i.

"My sorrows will be over when I find companionship in a cat."

Ahmad ibn Faris,
Iranian scholar and philologist (d. 1005)

"One cat just leads to another."
Ernest Hemingway, American author

ii.

There still wasn't enough snow on the ground for her to be able to tell if the smudgy, indistinct footprints clustered around the back entrance to her apartment were feline or from a skunk or a raccoon, but as far as she was concerned, cold-out was cold-out, and no night-roaming creature should have to go hungry, especially in the cold. So she added a bag of cat food, the cheapest kind the store sold, to her list. She was tempted to get the brand Yoda used to like, but she honestly couldn't remember the last time she'd even seen that kind on the shelves—Yoda had been gone for over ten years, and since then, she'd been so careful to avoid doing anything which might unexpectedly invoke his memory, she hardly ever walked down the pet food aisle anymore.

But the footprints convinced her that whatever it was out there, it might be hungry, and regardless of what sort of a creature it was, it apparently had decided to stick around *her* part of the house-turned-apartment complex.

And most small mammals could eat cat food...*I'll just make sure it's the cheapest kind*, she reminded herself, as she added it to the short grocery list written on a die-cut-cat-topped pad of paper with the inscription, "From the paw of...," under the orange cat's dangling left paw.

iii.

The smallest bag of cheap dry food she'd been able to find was still an arm-tiring three-and-a-half pounds, so she'd had to make frequent stops and starts on her way home that evening after work. But it was because of the weight of her cloth bag that she ended up stopping near one of those chips and candy vending machines next to the soda machine outside the hardware store. She vaguely recalled that the spot where the first vending machine now stood used to feature a live bait contraption (something so repulsive to her—living creatures waiting to be somehow scooped up and deposited at the bottom of a chute once some money was fed into the dollar-sucking slot—that she'd usually avoided standing anywhere near the thing), but now there was a new machine in its place…one with a hand-colored sign inserted in the spot where the chips and candy logo used to be.

"GENUINE 'TRASH BAGS'—WHY PAY MORE FOR A TRASH BALL WHEN YOU CAN GET A WHOLE BAG???"

She had heard of trash balls, those small clear plastic spheres filled with tiny tidbits of human offal, some mundane as a stubbed out cigarette, others as exotic as a foreign stamp still attached to picture postcard, or a tightly-folded dropped note found on a sidewalk. Some fellow over in Washington D.C. started selling them back around the turn of the century, and slowly they spread westward—when she and a co-worker from the bank went to St. Paul-Minneapolis for a seminar, she'd seen a trash ball machine outside a dry cleaners. True, she'd received only a folded up cigarette pack for her quarter, but it was a Canadian brand she'd never heard of before, and there *were* worse ways to blow a quarter.

But whoever bought this old snack machine and re-purposed it as a trash bag vendor had gone the traditional trash ball machines one better—s/he had affixed bits of paper to the outside of each bag (with said bags being recycled themselves, some from fast food joints, others from established stores), which gave a teasing indication of what might be inside. Most were standard emoti-cons, ranging from smiles followed by question marks, to clowns, what looked to be an Elvis, a Pope-icon, and even LOL's...but one was far more intricate, and specific, than the rest:

```
("–"-/").__. .—' '" -._.
6_ 6 ) -. ) -. -. ____.)
.. (_ Y_;) '..---/ /-- ' ! ; -..--- '
( i i), -" -- ( i i) , ' ((! . – '
```

Plus whatever was inside was covered by a bag from one of those Big Box pet-food/supplies only places, which was crudely stapled shut along the folded-over top. The bag was positioned behind a marker labeled "C-9"—she appreciated the additional association ("C" for cat, "9" for nine lives), and reflexively dug around in the coin pocket of her Burberry plaid wallet for a couple of quarters....

iv.

Once she found an old plastic margarine container which wasn't too high, she poured out a couple of cups worth of the "X"-shaped dry food into it, then placed it partway under the decrepit back deck attached to the house where she lived—the people who'd built it had done a half-assed job, and most of the lattice work around the base of the deck was either missing or badly weather-damaged, so she was able to shove the makeshift bowl of food about half a foot under the deck. Just so whatever it was that was coming around could eat under the cover of the deck floor, rather than out in the open. It might have been easier to use one of Yoda's old cat dishes, but she'd buried his favorite one with him, and the others she'd given away to the animal shelter, along with his bleach-sanitized litter pan and bedding. His toys, she'd kept, save for the pink-and-green bizzy ball she'd also placed in his box, next to his body, the one whose little silver bell was gone.

She did consider taking her big blue 9-volt battery flashlight outside, to peer under the dirt-floored expanse of the deck, but if the creature leaving the footprints was a skunk, she didn't way to scare it by shining a light in its half-awake face. So she simply shoved the bowl of crunchy food under the deck, and made her way back inside her quarter of the subdivided house.

v.

Once her groceries were put away, and the bag of cat food placed under her sink, she finally allowed herself to open the cat-decorated bag she'd impulsively bought on the way home. It was heavy, and had something rectangular inside, that much she could tell from the feel of it once it had plopped down the vending machine chute, and landed in the chrome glass-shielded bottom receptacle. Now sitting on her counter next to the sink, under the clear bright light from that *we energies* gift box of energy-savings supplies (insulating tape, a water-sav'r shower head, and a couple of coiled bulbs), the bag's pet store logo shone garish, yet vibrant, in the dull, weathered confines of her paint-peeling-cabinets-and stained-formica kitchen, as if it somehow belonged in another *newer* place.

Telling herself, *Don't go getting excited about a bag full of cast-off junk from some Dumpster*, she nonetheless found herself peeling apart the stapled top of the bag with the same sort of anticipatory excitement she used to associate with birthday and Christmas gifts. Once the top was open, she could see the glint of something metal and glass inside, as well as numerous other small, oddly-shaped items—

—but she made sure she emptied the bag before actually taking stock of what was inside, not looking too closely at the things she laid out neatly across her gold-flecked white countertop until everything was positioned before her:

An empty frame, tarnished silver, but deeply embossed with a design of fish bones, small balls of yarn, and cat silhouettes, with a deep blue velveteen backing piece behind the smudged glass insert.

Bits of cut-out photographs, from the 1970s or so, since she hadn't seen that type of developing—one square white-rimmed picture to the right, roughly three-by-three inches, plus an extra bit of paper to the left; a rectangle marked with the words "One Picture to Keep, One to Share" over a scored smaller picture, more wallet-sized than the first—since she was in high school, back in the mid-70s. All the smaller pictures were gone, with just the slightly tufted remains of the two scored edges to indicate that something had been torn away, and each of the bigger pictures had

had the central images cut out, leaving tantalizing outside corners still bearing shiny bits of faded color. The remaining images were indoor shots, hinting at stuffed animals (all cats, from what she could make out), bedding, pillow corners, and only fragments of the wall-papered walls beyond (some sort of flowered pattern). The cut-out shapes varied—some were circles, others rounded-cornered rectangles, and one was a heart…and on the inside edges of the round part of the two halves of the heart-shape, she saw the remains of something black and triangular, very close to the inner cleft of the heart. From their position relative to each other, she finally figured out what had been left out of the heart-shaped picture—the tips of the cat's ears. Whoever owned these pictures had been cutting out pictures to fit in tiny frames, one of the heart-shaped. Perhaps it was a locket. Or one of those refrigerator magnet-frames. All the other images had been cut so as to include all of the cat, but the tips of the ears just wouldn't fit inside the heart.

Cat toys, well-batted and chewed: A quartet of bizzy-balls, minus the inner silvery bells, which had slipped out through a couple of broken slats in the over-all lattice-work shape of the balls; a rabbit-fur-covered mouse, dyed vivid purple, with a half-chewed-off tail; half of a snap-together catnip toy, in the shape of a fuchsia heart; and a beat-up hand-sewn toy cat, crafted of black-and-white material, with a flat face decorated with a magic-marker-drawn pair of eyes, nose, and five whiskers per side over a smiling mouth.

An old blue-lined pad of paper with a spiral binding, covered with random jottings on every other page or so—grocery lists, reminders to pay bills, and, toward the end, a self-penned song, which was to be "sung to the tune of 'B-I-N-G-O'," which ended with the ear-worn refrain:

> "—and Mongo was his name-o:
> M!
> O!
> N!
> GO!
> And Mongo was his name-o!"

The handwriting was fluid, feminine, and slightly old-fashioned, with capital letters far more ornate than anything she'd learned in grade school.

Seventies photo developing, and a cat's name gleaned from a classic 1974 comedy, *Blazing Saddles*. Which told her that this cat had to have been 1) male, and 2) probably *very* big. And he had black ears.

Plus, since almost forty years had passed since the pictures were taken (then carefully cut apart), and the toys were chewed, Mongo was as long gone as her Yoda.

Telling herself that she could use toothpaste to clean up the little silver frame, and maybe put a picture of Yoda in it, she swept the other things off the counter back into the bag, then re-folded the top, and set it next to the bag of cheap cat food under her sink.

Time to start making her supper....

vi.

Although she hadn't dreamed of it in many years, not since she'd had that same dream two nights in a row—something which had never before or since happened to her—about a reborn Yoda, who was now living in some high rise apartment in New York City, with a middle-aged couple who obviously weren't rich, but were comfortable enough to afford a carpeted cat tree for him, plus a nice self-standing metal cage in the middle of the living room, and even though the cat who was telling her silently in the dream that he was, indeed Yoda, wasn't a silvery gray stripe with disproportionately big ears, but instead a marmalade tomcat with relatively smallish ears, she didn't believe him at first, which was why she ended up dreaming exactly the same dream once again, *tonight* she had an even older dream, the passed-on-cats dream, one of the ones which used to feature Yoda, plus all the other cats she'd had during her life.

The setting was always the same, even if the cats who came to her changed: A grassy field, endless rolling ground with the hint of undulations under the thick verdant Kelly green grass, dotted with dozens upon dozens of cats, a multi-hued and shaped cloud of rolling, lying, kitty-yoga-licking, jumping and hunkering cats. Some of them were recognizable to her, others new, but between her and the cats was this thick brick wall, dark-chocolate-brown brick, with slightly weathered, going-to-powder *mousse*-brown mortar between the bricks, which were set about a dozen bricks thick across the top, and perhaps two dozen high. Just enough to keep her from comfortably climbing on top of the thick barrier, but not enough to prevent her from leaning close to the wall. And as she came closer, one or more of her former cats would jump up on the wall, and let her pet them. Once it was Brutus, he of the huge round cheeks and daintily scalloped white "shoes" along the bottoms of his front paws. Another time, pale tiger-striped Jezebel, and her brother Tigger. The last time she'd been there, it was Yoda, no longer crippled by that virus he'd caught in kitten-hood, no longer wiggling that undulating, back-and-forth wobbling walk, but as perfect as he was born to be, but his hoarse cry was the same.

And every visit she'd made to this place ended the same way—she would be petting her cat, and suddenly it would jump down, back onto the grass on the other side of that big, thick wall, and she'd try to hoist herself up but kept jackknifing her body against the hard sharp masonry side of the wall, until she'd plop down hard on her side of the wall, all the while looking at those cats—and then she'd wake up.

The Yoda dream was the last nocturnal visit she'd paid to the thick brick wall...a couple of years or so after that dream, she'd had the back-to-back identical dream of him living in New York City, and then, no more cat dreams.

But the night she bought herself the trash-bag filled with bits and scraps of the life of a cat named Mongo and his owner, she went back to the wall beyond the cat-place.

At first, all she did was look at the cats cavorting in the field. Too many of them to count, too many colors and shapes to categorize. Then, one of them broke free of the crowd, and came toward her—a dark shape, indistinct, but big, with curious small voids at the top of each ear, and the closer he came the less discernible he became, until the point where he jumped up on the wall, and all she saw was a black-and-white blur, as if she'd suddenly lost her close-up vision, and needed glasses—

Then she woke up, and the dream began to lose coherence, leaving only the memory of an approaching dark, leaping shape.

* * * * * * *

As she left her apartment, she saw that it had snowed a bit more during the night; the tracks leading to and from the deck were definitely feline this time. Big prints, with a large inner pad surrounded by well-spaced toes. Probably a tom. She'd have to look for signs of spraying, come first light. She didn't think the other tenants would like cat-piss on the sides of the building, especially come warm weather. The landlord never came around, but the others (a couple with a small child, a young man in his twenties who did all the lawn-mowing, and a middle-aged couple she hardly ever saw at all) might complain…but she didn't smell anything, as she knelt down to sprinkle a small margarine tub's worth of cat food into the half-empty bowl.

All during the day at work, her mind kept imposing the rhythm of what the previous owner of the contents of the trash-bag called "The Mongo Song" over every small, repetitious task she performed:

Counting out money to a customer—"Five ("M!"), ten ("O!"), fifteen ("N!") and twenty ("GO!"), there you go, sir—"

Making copies at the machine—with each forward slide of the newly printed pages into the side chute, her mind merrily chanted, "—and Mongo was his name-o!!"

And even going to the bathroom on her break, mentally counting out four sheets of paper, each one accompanied by a silently shouted out letter or two.

And as she walked home, each step became part of "The Mongo Song," left-M!, right-O!, Let-N!, right-GO!! It was so infectious, she almost didn't notice that the glass door of the trash-bag machine was open when she approached the hardware store, but something external—a slippery patch of ice under the thin coating of snow on the sidewalk—did make her pause, and do a jiggly, Yoda-like back and forth shimmy, which caught the attention of the young man who was filling the trash-bag machine with several freshly packed bags of litter.

"Hey, you ok Ma'am? You hit a slippery spot? Man, I hate it when that happens to me—" He didn't stop filling the machine from the front, but did turn his head to look her way as he spoke. He was a bit past college age, with a knit Packers cap pulled low over his head, just skimming the edges of his gold-hoop-adorned ears, and she thought he had a stud of some sort in his nostril *and* his left eyebrow, but didn't want to stare too openly at either of them. He needed a shave, but otherwise looked to be clean. His jacket was old, and patched with duct tape along the elbows, but his jeans looked fairly new, as did his athletic shoes.

Realizing that she had to say something she nodded and said, "I bought one of your bags yesterday. The one with the crouching cat on it—"

"Oh yeah, the Mongo bag. That damn song in the notebook's been running through my head ever since I folded the stuff in there. But the frame's worth a few bucks, if you can clean it up—"

"I did. With toothpaste," she found herself adding, but before she started a mindless jabbering conversation with a stranger (albeit a stranger she'd paid 50¢ to via his machine), she added, "You have a good idea, recycling like this. Good luck with it," and started to walk past him, but the young man suddenly added, "I found all that stuff outside the old people's apartment complex, across town. I get most of my merchandise from there—the person dies, the family only wants so much of their stuff, and the rest goes in the Dumpster out back. Good stuff, it's a shame to let it go to the landfill. I almost didn't put the parts of the old pictures in there, but I never saw prints with a spare attached like that—thought someone might enjoy seeing them. When did they used to print 'em like that, with a smaller one attached? I mean, I thought *maybe* you'd know," he added with an embarrassed grin, once he realized the ageist implications of his remark.

"Back in the 1970s," she smiled, and left with a small wave of her gloved hand in his direction.

Behind her, the young man yelled, "Thanks...and hope you enjoy the Mongo."

Hearing him use the word like that, she remember that "Mongo" was also a term for things which were found and reused; she'd read a book review about the whole Mongo recycling phenomenon years ago in a *New York Times Book Review* at the library. What the snobby sorts in the Midwest sneeringly referred to as Dumpster-Diving, genuinely erudite types on the East Coast lovingly called 'Mongo," and pursued the gathering of cast-off treasures with total enthusiasm.

Yes, she mentally answered the young man, *I am enjoying the Mongo...the cat* and *the "stuff."*

The little ditty Mongo's owner had composed for him decades ago may have been an earworm, but it kept the drone of the bank's annoying *muzak* out of her head, even if the cat dream her small stash of Mongo goods had provoked had been a bit on the disturbing side.

She hadn't seen the cat-wall-place in so long, she'd begun to think it didn't exist anymore, even in dreams.

vii.

While her dinner was cooking in her small toaster oven, she sat at the counter, perched on one of the two mismatched bar stools she used for kitchen chairs, and began reading the small spiral-bound notebook from the trash-bag. There was no name in there, but the owner had to have been a woman; there was a reminder on one page to buy some sanitary napkins, and on another, she'd jotted down an appointment for a mammogram out at the clinic. Plus she'd put both dry and soft cat food on every list she made. Once, she added catnip, and another time, wormer pills. But among the lists and appointment reminders, she'd printed the word "BASTET" followed by this inscription:

> "An Egyptian cat-god, with a human body and a feline head."

The next page had a brief run-down of what ancient Egyptian families did when a cat passed on, including the fact that they shaved off their eyebrows in honor of the fallen feline. There was a crude drawing of a cat-shaped mummy, too.

She wondered if the long-departed Mongo was sick, or aging, when his owner wrote those things. Thinking of the unknown cat with the black ears (*he's big, really huge, and he was jumping up to greet* me *in that dream*—) made her think of Yoda, who'd lived an amazing fifteen years despite his difficulty walking and jumping (he really couldn't jump like a normal cat, but grabbed with his front paws and clawed his way onto the couch or the bed), and since that wasn't something she liked to think about, she turned her attention back to the scribbling of Mongo's owner.

Apparently Mongo had white paws; there was an aside about his "sock feet" and "strawberry pads," something the woman found worthy of note in her little spiral-bound notebook. She found herself wondering if he was a Tuxedo cat, or a Harlequin, with the half-white/half-black center stripe up the middle of his face. She'd always been partial to Tuxedos herself, and since every Tuxedo she'd seen had white feet, she decided that the owner of the left-over ear-tips had to have been a Tuxedo. Not that it really matter-mattered, but it was a thought which pleased her as she ate her single-serving plate of spaghetti and meatballs.

He probably had big feet, she told herself, thinking of the paw prints outside the deck, and wondering if the bag of food she'd bought the day before would last out the rest of the winter, or if the cat even liked it, despite obviously eating it.

Looking out the window near her back door, after she'd finished her dinner, she thought she saw a dark shape dart under the deck, but didn't want to turn on the light, lest it run off without eating. But it did look big, male-cat big. *Mongo*-big, like that huge galoot of a cowboy in that rather dated but still sort of funny movie from the seventies.

And when she went to bed, later that night, she told herself to dream that dream again, but forgot to remind herself to *remember* it, too....

viii.

More paw prints, going to and from the deck; she saw them as she left the apartment for work the next morning. If she'd dreamed, she couldn't recall it, but there was always that Mongo-song, echoing just under each and every thought, giving her steps an added bounce, and each thumbed-out bill slapped on the marble countertop at the bank an added flourish. Those five letters echoed behind every word she heard, and as she hurried home that evening, every step was in rhythm with the cadence of that long-forgotten/newly-remembered cat song, but as she neared her apartment, something else bounced along in her mind as she walked, something more than just a silly but catchy little jingle, an ode to a long-gone cat—she began to see images of Mongo, first the white middle of his Tuxedo face, then big green eyes, then the rest of him, all black save for his white feet, and as she crossed from the business section of town into the residential part of the same street, she found herself first silently, then not-so-silently mouthing the words of that nonsense song, her breath puffing out whitely before her lips:

> *"I had a cat and that was that,*
> *And his name was Mon-go—*
> *M!*
> *O!*
> *N!*
> *GO!*
> *And his name was Mong-o!"*

She remembered that she used to sing to Yoda, too, just nonsense syllables, rhyming his name, anything to attract his attention. But she never wrote down any of the words, silly as they were, to the Yoda songs, so they seeped from her memory, until nothing was left but the faint memory of having sung them.

Yoda, who'd been so unique, so trying because of his walking problems, but so much a part of her life, that once he was gone, she was afraid to even try to replace him, because no other at would be as *perfectly* unique as he was, due to his disability, yet also despite his imperfection, too.

"—And his name was Mong-oh!" she found herself panting as she approached her back-of-the-house entrance, and as she rounded the corner of the deck, she saw a dark shape dart under the silvery-faded wooden structure, but when she heard the sound of crunching, a noise she'd almost forgotten along with her Yoda-songs, something made her hunker down and whisper to the cat under deck, "I had a cat, and that...was that—"

The crunching stopped, and a head poked out from under the edge of the deck. It was still light enough out, despite the setting sun, to see that the cat was black, with a stripe of white down the middle of its face, and as it emerged from under the base of the deck, she saw that it was big, Mongo-big, with four white feet. It wasn't afraid of her, so it wasn't a feral, but it was slightly wary of her, not coming too close, but sitting just beyond arm's reach on the snowy concrete leading up to the deck steps.

"And who are *you*? Do you belong to anyone? You don't have a collar so I don't *think* anyone owns you... do they?" She found herself automatically slipping into that affectionate sing-song voice she used to use with Yoda, and with all her other cats, and the cat watched her intently, but didn't move forward, until she began to sing, "—and his name was Mongo...M!-O!-N-GO!... and *Mongo* was his name-o!" and when he heard the word "name-o" the cat came close, and began rubbing against her legs. And followed her up the steps and into the apartment, where he leaped up onto the counter and began dancing back and forth on the gold-dotted white formica, his sleek black-and-white body moving so quickly she didn't notice until after she'd poured him some more cat food into a shallow bowl that he was beautiful, but just slightly flawed—either he'd been in a fight, or had been frostbitten, but the triangular tips of both black ears were missing. Not that it mattered though; she thought he was beautiful, just as he was.

ix.

Bastet smiled.

In memory of all the other cats of mine, on the other side of the great wall. Including Mongo, who left me after one year and three weeks, on 11-29-08.

AFTERWORD

There was once a Yoda, and a Mongo, and both are dead now. Yoda lived to be fifteen-years-old, despite a myriad of physical problems, and yes, I did have a dream (had it twice, something I otherwise don't do) about him being reborn in New York City, as an orange tiger cat. Mongo…Mongo was a cat I had for a year and three weeks; he'd been a stray, but also a loving, friendly, beautiful homeless boy who shared his life with me for far too short a time. I took many pictures of him; he loved the camera and would start posing when I brought it out. He did look like the cat in this story, down to the missing tips of both ears (and no, he wasn't a trap/fix/release cat; he wasn't neutered, but apparently lost both ear tips to frostbite). And when he died of kidney failure, it just about killed me. My immune system took a nosedive and I had my first flares of gout in my hands the following spring, plus numerous other physical signs of deterioration. I still cry every time I think of him, over five years since he passed on. I keep wondering if I did the right thing, taking him in, if maybe he'd have lived longer if I never laid eyes on him. I don't know why he became ill so suddenly, but his death still haunts me.

I wrote this before he died, back when I had hopes of him being with me for years; I divided it into nine sections, one for each of a cat's lives. I had had the last line in mind for years, for a story I didn't even have mapped out—I just thought it was the perfect coda for a cat story. But I don't think Bastet, or any god for that matter, has ever smiled on me.

I also dreamed of the Great Brick Wall; others may believe in the Rainbow Bridge, but I have dreamt of the GBW several times, with different cats behind it. The GBW is exactly as I described it in my story; those dreams have one added dimension virtually none of my other dreams share—usually the only senses I "feel" in dreams are sight and sound. But I have felt the texture of the GBW, so I hope against hope that it might be out there…and beyond it, all my cats. Perhaps, when I die, I will be able to climb up over it at last.…

THE CAT-TRACKER
LADY OF ASAD ALLEY

Because she had no human relatives, the Cat-Tracker Lady of Asad Alley had listed me as her "next of kin" on the tiny bi-fold business card from one of the local funeral homes, which she kept in her wallet next to her green Wisconsin Non-Driver ID, the one which firmly stated that she was *not* an organ donor, nor did she wish to make any sort of anatomical donation after her death.

By the time the hospital where she was taken after she was found lying face down near one of the Dumpsters which lined Asad Alley called me, the organ donor vultures had come and gone, *sans* their little foam coolers filled with dry ice and human carrion. The nurse-receptionist-what*ever* who called me actually managed to insert that into her conversation with me that morning, "—and what's *really* sad is that Ms. Quies wasn't an organ donor, what with her being found alive...she seemed healthy otherwise... just such a shame—"

"You don't know who she *was*, do you?" I snapped, while trying to remove the snap-on plastic lid from my *latté* one-handed, and cradling the office phone against my ear with the other hand. Over four bucks for a cup of coffee, and they forget to put enough sweetener in there—even as the reality of Areille Quies' death bloomed in my mind like a slow-spreading stain on a napkin placed over a spill of java on a countertop, I found myself stubbornly clinging to the personal, the mundane, the ever-so-slightly annoying problem of a *latté* that just wasn't sweet enough…anything to make the news stay at bay, even for a few more seconds—

"Well, she only came in a couple of hours ago, and we just found the card with your contact info on it, but her name is on—"

"Areille Quies was the Cat-Tracker Lady…or didn't anyone notice the cat fur all over her coat? Do you ever read the papers, check out the Internet? She was all over the news…she had *Toxoplasma gondil* in her system. That's why she couldn't donate her organs, or sell blood. Her blood was infected, and so were her organs—"

"She wasn't wearing a Medic-Alert bracelet, so we didn't—"

"I don't think they *sell* them for *toxo*—besides, did you notice her age? She was a little past organ donating age—"

"Oh, we take organs from people older than she was…they're considered high-risk, but some people are willing—"

The lid on my cup wasn't budging, and that perky twerp on the other end of the phone wasn't about to even consider the possibility that anyone who came into the hospital with a pulse but no brainwaves wasn't prime organ procurement material. No wonder people got rabies and HIV from homeless donors. Taking a less-than-sweet sip, I mentally counted to five, and said, "*Forget* about the organ donation…do you know when I can collect her remains? Ms. Quies had very specific funeral arrangements planned in advance with us—"

"Oh she did?" I could picture the disappointed flap and downward flutter of the vulture's wings as yet another chance at the dead body was denied. "Usually in a case like this, the body is donated to science, y'know, for dissection—"

"What-time-can-I-pick-her-up?"

"Oh, any time after the doctor signs off on her… we've been busy here, and—"

"I will be there—and she better be there, too. In one piece," I snarled, before putting down the receiver with a hollow plastic clatter. Around me, the other volunteers at Friends of Feral Cats sat motionless behind their small desks, hands poised over keyboards, necks craned my way. Finally, that intern from the veterinary college, Ursula Something Or Other, said softly, "Don't tell me that Areille's—"

"I don't have to tell you then," I said through a sudden welling of phlegm and tears in my throat, before picking up my purse and slinging it over my shoulder, and exiting the Feral Cat Rescue and Rehabilitation Society's headquarters, leaving my half-consumer *latté* on my desk. Behind me, I heard the other speaking softly and a couple of people started crying, but I couldn't pay attention to them, not if I wanted to drive myself to the hospital a couple of miles away, in the downtown section of the city.

Areille had gone out that morning on the same mission which consumed her life for the past thirty-some years—to feed her feral cats, in that alleyway behind Asad Avenue, where all the Muslim shops and restaurants were located in the loosely-configured Middle Eastern conclave in the southeast part of the city. The businessmen there welcomed her presence; being part of a religion whose founder was an ardent cat-lover, they helped her buy the food she lugged to the alleyway each morning in two stained and slightly smelly cream-colored cloth shopping bags, and since she claimed that a well-fed cat was a better mouser/ratter than a starving animal, no one who frequented the numerous establishments fronting Asad Avenue ever had reason to complain about rodent droppings in their food, or heat-seeking rats rubbing against their legs while they waited for their ride at the open-fronted bus stop in front of The Emerald Crescent Bookstore.

And since all the restaurants donated their left-overs to either a homeless shelter or a farmer's co-op (the latter took the scrappy-scraps, for animal feed for chickens and pigs, even though the latter was a forbidden food among devout Muslims—Areille once told me that she figured the restaurateurs got around this by rational-izing that their donations to the local porcine population was a way of "giving back" after all the bad feelings over 9-11; Areille was like that, making slightly paranoid remarks about just about everything…she was the one who used to call the organ procurement folks "vultures" toting "human carrion" in their little BioHazard foam coolers), that left nothing for the feral cats to eat besides the mice and rats which just might be contaminated with poison. Or so Areille often said, as she'd put out the fresh aluminum pie pans on the ground near the center-most cluster of Dumpsters, then wait for her feral friends to come running out of their hidey-holes all along the alley, before pouring her special mixture of dry cat food, chopped up hot dogs, and—once a month only—wormer paste mixed with people-tuna, onto the round pans. Working for an agency which supported the care and population control of feral cats throughout the Midwest, I was used to seeing people who fed alley cats, but there was something about Areille Quies which was just a bit different. No one else was able to make the cats literally dance for their dinner. That was what brought her to the attention of Friends of Feral Cats in the first place; some Dumpster diver looking for aluminum cans happened to catch the dinner *matinée*, and made a video of the event on his camera phone, which was seen by someone who had access to YouTube, and one it was downloaded onto the Internet, people started sharing it and, eventually, someone emailed me and said:

U –Must– check this out!!

Everyone in the office who saw the clip thought it had to be photo-shopped—there was this older woman in a dirty-looking red-and-black parka, standing there in an alley next to a chained-shut Dumpster, surrounded by cats...all of whom were standing on their hind legs, front paws paddling the air before them, like feline sleepwalkers, and one by one, she'd hold their paws and sway in place with them, in a lurching two-step, then another cat would gingerly trot forward, to repeat the pattern.

People started to leave messages on the boards when the clip was shown, and eventually someone wrote that this was "—NOT—a fake, I've seen this woman myself, BTW" and then another person left a message consisting of a time and a location, and the next morning, I was there, waiting in the chilly February slush of snow and tire-plowed grime at the mouth of the alley behind Asad Avenue. The woman in the grimy parka nodded at me as she shuffled into the alley, shoulders bent low as she lugged the cloth bags filled with something obviously heavy and round-shaped into the alley proper. Up close, I realized that she was at least in her fifties, perhaps older—it was hard to tell for certain, since she had a flushed-ruddy face with plump cheeks and a nose whose dark pores resembled the flesh of an unripe strawberry. Once she was in front of that same chained Dumpster from the YouTube video clip, she set down her bags, and extracted several pie pans, which she proceeded to place roughly ten feet apart, before starting at the far end, and hunkering down to examine the snowy asphalt, moving so quickly yet so clumsily, I couldn't help but remember that scene in *Fargo* when the hugely pregnant Chief of Police Marge Gunderson suddenly squatted down near that overturned car on the frozen lake and announced "…I think I'm gonna barf!"

I wanted to laugh, but something warned me that doing so would somehow spoil what was about to happen next. Thirty feet away, the woman began craning her hooded head first in one direction, then in another, before saying softly, "*There* you are," and after she spoke, the cats began to ooze from the alley, a wiggling ocean of low-slung bodies, their fur rippling wave-like as they moved in a huge phalanx of long, lean backs, lowered tails, and flattened-eared heads, coming closer and closer to the woman as she went from pan to pan, not leaving food, but merely indicating that the pans were, indeed, there. Realizing that she'd been looking for their tracks in the foot-print and truck-tire patterned alley-snow, I continued to watch quietly, my breath coming in short air-whitening hitches, as she returned to the central Dumpster, and said, "Who's gonna dance with me?"

Then it began to happen—the cats rose up, tsunami-like, backs suddenly pitched upwards, front paws lifted, heads pointed chin-forward in her direction, tails out straight behind for balance, and one-by-one, they approached her, walking gingerly on their hind feet alone, as first a huge black male with dainty scallops of white on his front toes came toward her, and she took his paws in her leather-mittened hands, and they executed a lumbering, swaying dance, and once that big-headed tom was done, another cat—this one a black-and-white tuxedo—took his place, and so on, with orange and calico and tiger-stripe and solid gray partners taking turns with her, until all the cats had had their time on the dance floor with the woman... only then did she pick up the cloth bags, and extract big margarine tubs, each filled with food. Once she began feeding them, the cats acted like any other alley cat across America might act—they jostled each other for a better position by the pan, they hissed, they batted at each other with their paws, and finally, once all the food was devoured, they hurried off as one, an undulating retreating ebb-tide of cold-puffed furry bodies, going back to wherever it was they hid during the daytime.

I actually recognized a few of the cats, from some of our Trap & Spay Days promotions, when we passed out live traps to area businessmen, and fixed all the caught cats for free, just as long as the person who trapped them watched over them during the healing time after the animals were spayed or neutered. But there were always newcomers to the clutter of cats, abandoned or lost felines who somehow came to find outdoor life among their own kind preferable to life—and often certain death—in a shelter.

The woman started picking up the licked-clean pans, and while she was putting them in her bags, along with the empty margarine containers, I finally found myself asking her, "Do you do this every day?"

"Yeah…leap year day included. They expect it, and I like it, so…I come out here. The people who own the businesses here, they said I could—"

Obviously, someone had hassled her about her daily feeding in the past, probably those wonks down at City Hall. There wasn't any ordinance on the books against feeding strays, but that usually didn't stop the city workers from throwing their weight around, especially when it came to women. Being single myself, I'd had more than one run-in with those guys from City Hall over everything from pruning the trees which over-hung my sidewalk to how much water I did (or didn't) use each month, so I asked, "Anyone hassle you about this?" I pointed to the bags she carried. Stumbling in place slightly as she picked up the last of the pans, she said without turning to look my way, "Oh, the usual suspects…cops, city drones, tourists. The owners, they pay for what I feed them, so I keep coming. Gotta get my cat fix," she added enigmatically, before heading for me, bags bouncing off her black jeans-covered thighs, her face ruddy from the cold and from the effort of breathing hard and shallow.

"'Cat fix'—?"

"I suppose you could call me a crazy cat lady without the cats. I used to be able to have my own cats, but between the Toxo and the umpteen bouts of cellulitis, the doctors at the clinic said if I keep a cat and it bites me again, I could die. They said I have some sort of feline bacteria, something with a 'c', all through my blood, right down to the marrow. It flares up if I get a bite or bad scratch. Which is why I have to wear these—" She held up her hands, and showed me the thick leather mitts which extended down past her wrists, well into her elasticized jacket sleeves, adding matter-of-factly, almost by rote, "—just in case one of these kitties claws me or tries to bite. I have duct tape wrapped around my one pair of socks, around my ankles, in case I have to try to kick apart a cat fight. Last time one of my own cats bit me, it was on the front of my left foot. I had on two pairs of socks on account of it being cold in my apartment, but he still sunk in two fangs. Took a lot of iodine to get rid of *that* one, but it didn't heal for weeks. I just couldn't afford another visit to the hospital. So once the last of mine passed on…I started coming here. I saw their tracks, one morning. Too many for just one cat, so I left them some food…one of the shop owners saw me, and I thought he was going to hassle me, but he started in on some story about his prophet's cat once falling asleep on his sleeve, and rather than wake the cat up he cut off the sleeve, and then I knew it was ok, that I could feed the cats. These people, they like cats. Not dogs, but cats…they don't like *worship* them, the way the Egyptians used to, but they're good about them, and me feeding them. Now they give me some money, to help feed them—"

She kept on talking, without ever asking my name that first day, and I realized that she had to be isolated, given her eagerness to overshare with a complete stranger. I didn't get a chance to ask her her name that day, but I did learn it, when she paused in mid-ramble to pull a small Burberry plaid wallet out of one pocket, and slid out her non-driver ID, which had her name and really bad photo of her on it.

"—every time I go in they give me grief over not putting an organ donor sticker on my card, but that wasn't as bad as the first time I went in for a card, and this guy at the DMV, some fat slob with a greasy black comb-over, asks me, 'Are you a retard? You're too young to be getting a non-driver ID, and the only people your age who get them are retarded, so what kind of retard *are* you?' and I tell him 'I've got a degree, but I'm also dyslexic, and I have no depth perception, so *that's* what "kind of retard" I am' and the guy shut up, but he kept giving me dirty looks anyway—"

I realized that dyslexia and stereo blindness weren't Areille Quies' only problem—it wasn't until my fifth visit to the alley that she told me about the *Toxoplasma gondil* parasitic infection which she'd apparently caught while still in her teens or early twenties, when she was actually an honor student in high school and college (after the tenth visit, she let me follow her to her apartment, where I saw the framed High Honors high school diploma, and the *Magna Cum Laude* BS in English she'd received over thirty years before from local schools, which shared wall space with literally thousands of individual images of the hundreds of cats she'd had over the years, all grouped in multi-image-matted picture frames of a dozen different finishes and designs), but which didn't fully manifest itself in the usual symptoms of slowed reflexes, immunity to the scent of cat urine, or the surreal attraction to all things feline until she was close to thirty. It was then that she kept on having so many car accidents that she lost her license for good, then began losing even the most menial of jobs, until disability kicked in around the time she reached Social Security age, and she was able to devote herself to her true life's work—caring for he cats whose print she'd been tracking down Asad Alley.

By the time I was able to enter her cave-like apartment, with its walls covered from ceiling level to about a foot off the floor with countless photo montages, interspaced with cheaply framed pictures of cats torn from old calendars, permanently closed drapes, and the legions of stuffed cats of both domestic and wild form, she had agreed to let me write an article about her, for the newsletter FoFC published every four months for those who donated money to the organization, but the city paper eventually reprinted that piece, along with some still pictures of the Feeding Dance, and single-frame images of the walking cats themselves. Donations for The Friends of Feral Cats went up after the original piece ran in the newsletter, and they poured in once the story was reprinted, then virtually threatened to clog our P. O. Box to the point where the Postmaster tried to make us rent a bigger box once one of the national news organizations picked up the story.

As I waited for a red light to change at an intersection two blocks away from the hospital where Areille's body had been taken that morning, after she'd been found mugged and apparently whacked on the head with some blunt object—her empty bags gone, but her wallet untouched, which the organ-vulture at the hospital told me led the police to consider this some sort of anti-animal hate crime—I found myself remembering what Areille had said about all the attention my article had brought her.

"The money people give to the shop owners to give to me is fine, but you'd think they'd want to take the cats home, give them someplace good to live. In a garage, or a barn. Now if these guys were special, like that bald cat that was born at that farm, the one they bred into the Sphinx breed, or those mutant kitties with the short legs people breed on purpose now, people would be coming here in droves to trap them and take them home. But all they do is beg for their supper…and once one of them let me dance with him, the others just started to do it, too. Now if they did it for everyone, *then* they'd find homes—"

The light turned, and I finished the trek to the hospital. There was paperwork to sign, and luckily I didn't have to talk to Organ Vulture Woman, but some male resident, and a beat cop who'd been one of the first to find Areille Quies' body. Since she'd been getting on in years, Areille had been sure to mention FoFC in her will, even though she had next to nothing in terms of property to leave us, but her main reason for leaving that pittance to us was so that I'd be sure to carry out her final wishes…which I was careful *not* to spell out to the resident or the officer I spoke to that day. All they knew was that her body was to be taken to a local funeral home for cremation. It was something she was adamant about; she feared that her infected blood might somehow make its way into the groundwater, or the water supply itself, if she was to be embalmed, and given the toxic state of her tissues, a green, no-embalming burial was also out of the question for her. But cremation…that was thorough, and sanitary. Once she was ashes, her gradually-acquired fear of tainting other living beings was a moot point.

"I was wondering…when they're developed, could I please see the photos of the crime scene? I knew Ms. Quies for a few years, and I'd just like to know what happened—"

The cop stopped to scratch his close-cropped head under his hat, and began shaking his head no, but did say, "We think it was a pipe, or maybe a bat which was used. But at least she wasn't bloody…judging from the paw prints all around her, the cats must've licked off all the blood. Probably hungry, although why they didn't bite her, I dunno—"

A small spidery shiver or remembrance, as ethereal as walking into a cobweb and feeling it lightly pull-then-release against my skin, rippled through me, as I recalled one of the many mostly one-sided conversations I'd had with Areille (her doing most of the talking, as was her wont—if it didn't have to do with cats, she just zoned out), when she was telling me about her *Toxo* diagnosis, and what she found out about it on her own:

"I read in a newspaper, or maybe it was a magazine, about something the Center for Disease Control and Prevention said about people who contracted *Toxo*— we're more likely to be eaten by cats than other people. The article or blurb or whatever it was I read said that over 60 million people have it, too...you'd need a lot of cats to get busy eating if what they said is true. The cat food companies would go out of business for sure. But I suppose they meant that we're more likely to have a bunch of cats, so if we die in the house, and can't feed them, well, they'll take matters into their own paws. Or maybe we smell better to cats, on account of having the *Toxo*. They say that the lifespan of the *Toxo* parasite starts in the cat, then it makes its way to the human or animal, then it's supposed to get back to the cat to survive, which means the parasite has to go to the brain, so that the cat can eat it...which sounds crazier than the crazy cat lady disease, but that's what I read, anyhow. In some magazine or something."

Wishing I'd known her before the *Toxo* began to erode her mind at the edges, leaving her thoughts as vaguely connected as strands of thread in a lace doily, I'd nodded, and started to try to change the subject when she'd added, while cutting up the *kosher* hot dogs one of the butchers on the avenue used to give to her into small bite-sized chunks on an old wooden cutting board shaped like a whale, "After I'm cremated, I don't want my ashes put in an jar, or scattered in the wind...I want them mixed in with the cat's food, for one last meal—a goodbye dinner, with me as the main course. Remember the end of that science fiction novel, *Stranger in a Strange Land*? When that man who was raised on Mars dies, and they all eat his ashes in a meal? I read that in college. My professor, he was a Catholic and didn't approve, but I thought it was so perfect. Beats getting flying ash in your eyes—remember *The Big Lebowski*? His friend Donny in the coffee can—"

Remembering that scene in the film Areille had spoken about that day, and visualizing Jeff Bridges' The Dude covered in cremains out on that windswept ocean-side dune, I began giggling, but the cop and the doctor only took my reaction as a natural one to the horror of Areille's last minutes in the alley, with her body covered with cats, all jockeying to get a taste of her blood, and nodded sympathetically at me, before patting me on the shoulder, and telling me how sorry they were for my loss.

I nodded without saying anything, all the while thinking that I'd need to go out really early in the morning after the cremation, just in case this same cop caught me feeding human cremains to the animals....

* * * * * * *

By the time I'd authorized the release of her remains to the designated funeral home for the prepaid cremation, the afternoon edition of the paper was out, and in the Local News section, there was a short piece about Areille's death, which referenced my article for pull quotes. They used one of the archive images of her dancing with the cats, and the reporter who wrote the piece mentioned that the cats would go hungry until someone else took over for her, and finished with the line:

> "Their dance cards no longer full, the feral cats of Asad Alley will be sitting out not only this dance, but all the dances to come."

Not bad, given the short notice, but as I continued to read the rest of the paper, while waiting in the lobby of the funeral home, I told myself, *I don't know if they'll like their new partner, but* my *dance card's empty....*

* * * * * * *

Once I was in the alley the next morning, having done a limbo duck-and-slide under the yellow crime scene tape still fluttering in the cold pre-dawn wind, I found myself doing what Areille had done each morning— dropping clean pie tins on the snowy ground, then peering for cat tracks along the walls of the alley. On the spot where she had been hit and injured, someone— one of the Muslims, perhaps?—had placed some cold-withered flowers wrapped in butcher paper. But there was no blood staining the snow...just an overlapping mash of cat and human footprints. Not expecting that the feral cats would come running out for me, I began scooping out huge globs of cat food mixed with cat lady ashes onto the plates—Areille wasn't a very big woman, but there were still so many cremains that I ended up leaving about a dozen plates in that alley, each topped with a mound of canned cat food (which I'd bought the evening before) and Areille. Telling myself that it was what she specifically wanted, even if it was bizarre beyond even crazy cat-lady crazy, I hurried for the mouth of the alley, eager to quit that narrow dark space before the cats either attacked the food (something I really didn't want to see or hear) or attacked me, but as I was bending over to slide under the flapping ribbon of yellow-and-black tape, I heard this odd sound—a rhythmic pad-pad-pad susurrus, of something hard and small hitting slightly yielding ground, and even though I didn't want to, I found myself turning around to take a look.

First, all I could see were the luminous backs of the cats' eyes, wavering yellow-green dots, small-veined and oddly high above the ground. Then, as they came closer, I realized why their street-lamp-reflected eyes were so oddly positioned.

They were walking. On their hind paws, front feet held up in the begging position in front of them, and slowly, quietly, they settled in groups before the pans of food I'd left, and before they hunkered down to eat, they danced around the tins, heads held up high, chins skyward. As if Areille was holding their paws in turn....

Wishing I hadn't left my cell phone at home (one look at the voice mail list of reporters who wanted quotes from me made me shut it off the night before), I could only watch, camera-less, as the cats did their dinner dance, backs arched proudly in the dim light, until the smell of the cat food came wafting down the alley, and I hurried away from there....

Once I'd spoken to all the reporters who'd left messages, I felt as if I'd absorbed a part of Areille Quies as surely as if I'd been a cat partaking of that final meal with her. Eventually, interest in the murder (which was eventually solved; the cop at the hospital was right, it was a group of cat-haters who ironically also belonged to a local bird-watchers organization) died down, the Muslim business owners got together and fed the cats on their own, and gradually, the everyday business of getting back to my life as a Friends of Feral Cats worker took over my thoughts. I'd made Ursula What's-Her-Face go through Areille's apartment and photograph all her stuff for eBay, per Areille's request (amazingly, everything, even her high school and college diplomas, sold, with the proceeds going to FoFC), and soon it was spring, then summer, and I was certain that the whole Areille-in-the-Alley part of my life was over, done with, a sad/funny/surreal interlude...until the day when Ursula came into the office and demanded that we all log onto YouTube, to see a specific video—

Déjà vu washed over all of us as we watched the action which took place in the alley behind Asad Avenue, obviously filmed with a cell phone camera, but this time, the only thing missing was Areille herself, as the cats danced and walked and stayed upright in that alley and gradually other people, the Muslim shop owners and their customers, entered the alley, too, but the cats kept on their feet, and danced willingly with

whomever was brave enough to extend their hands...
and while I recognized some of the cats from the time
when their original partner was alive, many of the
other cats were young, little more than kittens, and the
people in the alley had to bend down quite low to dance
with them, but all of them were smiling, and silently
laughing and clapping their hands to some unheard
song, as the cats kept on dancing, and I kept doing the
feline math in my head, *Nine weeks gestation, plus five
months, maybe six equals whatever was in her blood
that morning did get into the cats after all...but I don't
think it was just* Toxo *they ingested.*

And when I saw one of the children pick up a kitten,
and carry it away, I remembered what she had said,
about the bald cat in that barn, and those mutant cats
with the tiny legs, and for the first time since the cat
tracker lady of Asad Alley died, I found myself wanting
to get myself to that alley, and dance with the first cat
who would walk up to me, and allow me to take his or
her paw in mine....

*Inspired by the life of Joseph Zeman, "the
pigeon man of Lincoln Square" (1931-2008),
and the articles of Barbara Mahany.*

*With thanks to James B. Johnson, who sug-
gested this story to me.*

*Dedicated to the memory of Grady, Quinn,
Sheba, Trudy, Baby Biscuit, Max, Mongo,
Ebony, Graykins, and Fluffer-Nutter.*

*And also The Dude, Harley, Inky, Bogie,
and Chickpea*

—A. R. Morlan (and cats) 2013

AFTERWORD

In some ways, this story is the distaff version of a later story in this collection, "No Heaven…," in that it is essentially a two-person dialogue concerning mortality, cats and otherworldly aftermaths of the deceased older person's demise. Like "No Heaven…," it is also based on the life of a real person, in this case Joseph Zeman, an elderly man who loved to feed pigeons, and who was beaten to death by bird-haters in the last decade. I read an article in *The Chicago Tribune* about him, and immediately recast it in terms of an old cat lady and her dependents. There's virtually nothing of Mr. Zeman in this story, however; while I do like pigeons, far more than most folks, I am more comfortable writing about my absolute favorite animal, the cat. Many of the details of the Cat-Tracker Lady's life are taken from my own existence; I literally can't give blood or donate my organs due to a constant load of bacterial infection in my blood (once, when an elderly cat of mine bit my finger, within less than eight hours I developed what a doctor called "a week's worth of infection" in that hand, and he also said if I hadn't come to the emergency room when I did, I would've been dead within a couple of days or so), plus I cannot drive, a fact which has caused me a great deal of ridicule and verbal abuse in this small town where I live/exist. Not being able to drive automatically makes me something of a freak; when I went to get my first non-driver ID back in the 1990s, the fellow at the DMV kept asking me, "What kind of a retard are you? No one our age gets these unless they're a retard."

I also feed stray cats, although never as many as my character. I've live-trapped some of them, and taken them home—one Momma Cat lived with me for twelve years, while others are too sick by the time I get them and don't live very long, but at least they are mourned when they pass, and given proper burials. I am one of those suckers who probably donates too much to animal welfare charities, but hey, I'm single, I have no kids, and who else is going to get the money once I'm dead, right? To me, there is nothing more perfect than a cat, and the fact that so many are living horrible lives in shelters or outdoors or in (worst of all) research labs just tears me up inside. I only wish that once I do pass, that my death could somehow make *all* the strays out there more adoptable, or better yet, somehow magically give all those cats a home. But I also know that fairy tales never, never, come true, nor do wishes, or hopes, let alone dreams. But it is still a thought, no matter how fantastical it may be....

There is lone last thing I wish to share in regard to this story—it was almost published in the *Cat Tales* anthology series edited by the late, great, and deeply-missed George Scithers, but the volume it would have been in was canceled. I even got a chance to correct galley pages for it, and *almost* had a chance to see it published, but it was not to be.

It was the last story I ever almost-sold; lately, I can

no longer even submit material to 99% of the magazines, anthologies, and e-books out there, due to being totally unable to work a computer (as it is, I struggle to type out a single sentence on a typewriter—it takes me hours to pound out something which might take another person minutes on a computer or even a typewriter). I've had to give up writing, after twenty-five years of consistently selling to over 130 different magazines, anthologies, and e-zines; it is a forced retirement, to be sure, and one which causes me many sleepless nights, but it is something I cannot overcome, nor can I change the publishing world, so I'm forced to stop doing the lone thing I was good at. That, perhaps, is why this story is special to me; unlike the main character, though, there is nothing that even my passing will do to benefit others....

THE CAT WITH
THE TULIP FACE

*"When it's time to die, let us not discover
that we have never lived."*

Henry David Thoreau

*For Sassy, with love,
And for Little Guy (1983-1988), in remembrance*

AUTHOR'S NOTE: This novelette is a prequel to my novel
The Amulet, and takes place in late 1986, a year before
the events in the novel.

Meaow.

"Kitty-kitty?" Arlene asked the humid early
morning air, as she glanced up and down Wisconsin
Street. Darkness welled in recessed shop doorways,
and gave an inky sheen to the large display windows.
The greenish-white street lamps were too far away to
cast much of a glow where she stood, midway between
the tacky novelty shop and the building which used
to be the Ewerton Savings and Loan but was now a
lawyer's office (*after* the Century 21 Realty office
came and went).

A fine mist settled on Arlene's exposed face and forearms; she rolled down the plastic backed canvas sleeves on her outsized slicker and tried calling again. "C'mon, Kitty-kitty. It's okay, I won't hurt you." She could hear the cat (kitten? It sounded young) crying, but the humidity in the sluggish July air made it difficult to pinpoint just where its cries originated.

Meeeaow!

Closer and louder now. Arlene walked forward slowly, heading toward the tiny diner that used-to-be-a-clothing-boutique to the north of her. In the distance she heard a truck's many wide tires snick-splash along one of the side streets behind her. At this hour of the morning—just before four—the only things moving on the streets of Ewerton were out of state truckers, the last stragglers coming home after an all-night party held in one of those walk-up apartments nestled above the department stores, the occasional stray animal— and Arlene.

Plastic mesh shopping bags in hand, Arlene had Ewerton all to herself in the mornings. She was the Queen of Ewerton Avenue, the Owner of Wisconsin Street. *And the Duchess of the Dumpsters*, she often joked with herself as she leaned into the back-of-the-store Dumpsters, her fingers sensitive to the feel of aluminum cans, the odd piece of discarded merchandise, or even the past-its-due-date box or carton of food.

And stray animals. Often, she'd unintentionally scare a wild cat or something smaller and quicker that she wasn't about to try to scrutinize in order to determine its species. And some mornings, she had footsore canine company for the length of a few blocks, until a slobbery tongue touched her hand in farewell and the empty streets rang with the sound of dog nails doing a chitinous tap-dance on the concrete.

But these had been animals, hungry, tired, or just plain lonely enough to allow Arlene to pick them up and scavenge them like an aluminum can, or an old box of breakfast cereal. Not that she thought of her pets as refuse, or cast-offs, though. Arlene treated all of her "finds" with respect, be they inanimate or animate. The aluminum cans were washed, then carefully crushed flat, prior to their storage in black plastic bags in the basement (and their subsequent return to the recycling truck come Thursday). The rust-dotted kitchen tools, chipped dishes, and one-left cards of kitchen magnets or corn-on-the-cob servers were diligently scrubbed, mended or matched with other odd-lot items waiting in Arlene's already cluttered kitchen drawers.

As for the animals…Arlene was a couple years short of being able to collect her own Social Security, but what with her late husband's SS checks, and the modest sum he'd left in the bank for her, she had just enough to pay her utility bills plus her considerable veterinarian bills. If a cat or dog needed food, she bought it name brands plus those expensive treats in the fancy little cans or boxes, while she ate weeks-old spareribs from the IGA dumpster. Should the animal need flea shampoo, she used only a half a tablet of denture cleaner in her chopper-hopper each day. When she wrote out the checks for her animals' shots each year, she *didn't* write out a check to cover the cost of her Ben-Gay and non-aspirin.

If you take it in, you take care of it. That thought alone was enough to banish any temptation to pamper herself. She had lived over sixty good years, years of plenty. *And I still have plenty*, she stubbornly told herself many a morning. *Only difference is, I don't have to pay for all of it.* That some of her finds—the four-legged ones—ended up costing her money she really couldn't afford to spend so freely never fazed Arlene, living alone as she did, with no children or grandchildren—or even many friends, for that matter—Arlene considered the love of her "babies" payment in full, thank you. While she knew that she'd have to make the little she had last until her own SS kicked in, Arlene had long ago decided that a life lived without *giving*, to *someone*, wasn't a life.

Her years with Don had proved that to be a fact.

So there she was, an old woman with ridiculously thin ankles which vanished in a pair of velcro-strapped running shoes, walking briskly down the street, her good ear cocked and waiting for the next *Meaow*. She walked faster, both out of need and urgency. With the gradual lightening of the sky, it was urgent that she get home before the delivery trucks began to arrive at the stores, and the graveyard shifts at the sash and door and paper mill were let out. And she knew that that cat (kitten?) *needed* her.

Six years of combing the pre-dawn streets had taught Arlene that for a little animal, alone and scared, dawn is too late. With the coming of light come cars with drivers who speed up when they see something small and frantic trying to cross the street. Arlene had toed many a pulp-headed animal to the curb during her "normal" shopping hours.

But if she could find this cat before the coming of the light—

Meeeaow!

That was why it was hard to get a fix on its cries— they came from *above* Arlene. Looking up, she saw the kitten sitting on the high window ledge of the dentist's office close to the intersection of Wisconsin Street and Fourth Avenue East. That window set in the gray stone facade was a good five feet off the ground, a small window with a deep ledge, recessed enough for a tiny kitten to hunker down close to the glass.

"Aw, c'mon, kitty, you can come closer, I won't hurt you," Arlene coaxed, as she stood on tiptoes and reached for the kitten. At five foot four, she was just tall enough to brush the animal's silky coat with the tips of her blunt fingers. The kitten was warm, exceptionally so for an animal which had most likely been sitting on that ledge all night. Its fur was as fine-textured as washed silk; as the kitten breathed its fur undulated like wind-whipped draperies, a most peculiar sensation.

The kitten stopped crying, and edged closer to Arlene; two huge black ears surmounted a mottled white and black wedge of a face. It looked to be about three months old. In the spill of the street-lamp, Arlene noticed that the kitten's eyes were tiny, baby-like. They glittered against the surrounding white fur like pebbles in the bottom of a fish tank, all watery and rounded.

Then, as if it had sized Arlene up and found her satisfactory, the kitten jumped off the ledge into her waiting arms. Upon impact, it began to purr, a loud rumble that radiated from its chest outward, making the ribs and skin vibrate. Arlene undid the top snap on her slicker and tucked the kitten inside; as she did so, her fingers brushed against the base of the kitten's tail. Gonads the size of large peas filled the scrotum.

As she positioned her left arm under the kitten, Arlene thought, *Awfully big down there for such a tiny baby boy…must be older than I thought.* Arlene's bag of cans clunked against her leg as she walked, but soon the kitten's purr drowned out even that noise.

By the time she was halfway to her home on Polk Avenue, the kitten was kneading her stomach.

* * * * * * *

Not only was the kitten older than Arlene had first guessed, he was…*uglier* than she'd realized. When she first brought him home, she hurried past the cats and dogs winding around her legs and shoved the wiggling kitten into the bathroom; she dreaded having to give all ten of her animals flea baths just in case the new arrival was crawling with the little brown varmints. After dumping some food into a saucer (also scavenged, a little white bowl with a childish picture of a spaceman on the moon in the bottom), she opened the bathroom door long enough to shove the food inside and slammed it before the kitten ran out. (There were litter pans positioned all over the house, including the bathroom, so she wasn't worried about any accidents after the kitten ate.) But she didn't get a good look at her newest find until after she'd fed her other friends, then brewed a cup of Earl Gray for herself.

While the other animals whined, scratched, hissed, and panted outside, Arlene quickly opened the door and slipped into the bathroom. The kitten was sitting on the toilet tank, in a Sphinx pose. Sitting sideways on the toilet seat, her back to the bathtub, Arlene said as she stroked the kitten's seal-sleek fur, "Gracious, you are the most *awful* looking kitty I've seen yet." The kitten blinked a kitty-kiss at her and began purring, as if she'd just said he was the most beautiful animal in the universe.

The kitten's capacity for affection wasn't in keeping with his appearance; not only were his ears *way* too big, so huge they almost met in the center of his upper head, but his face was all…wrong.

The too-small green eyes were only the beginning. The kitten's forehead and nose were all of one line, unbroken by dips, bumps, or anything. Just a straight slope from the too-close ears down to the nose leather. Arlene's cats, while not purebreds, were similar to each other in that their noses all dipped down parallel to their eyes in a pleasing sloping "S" curve. Years ago,

Arlene had a cat named Louie who closely resembled an Oriental Shorthair, and even *his* nose had had a slight dip to it.

But the kitten's nose resembled something drawn with a straight-edge. Head-on he looked even worse, for his white face was marred in the middle by an irregular blotch which completely obscured his nose, leather and all. When Arlene glanced at him fast, it, almost seemed that he had no nose at all. And his tiny, slightly bulging eyes didn't add to his beauty, either.

Gently pulling back the kitten's gums, she said, "Just want to check your teeth...*good* boy." Wiping off cat spittle onto her smock top, Arlene frowned to herself. This kitten had his canines. Top and bottom, almost fully grown in. Which made him..."Hum, lemme *see*—I found Guy-Pie when he was about five months old, and he had *his* canines" (not to mention over a hundred fleas which Arlene had drowned in a jelly-jar glass) "so you're pretty close to that age, aren't you?"

The kitten purred in agreement. Arlene patted his sides; the ribs stood out like the tines of a serving fork held an inch above a table. Pitiful. The skin was sucked in close to his rump and guts, and his stifle bones felt like marbles under Arlene's hard fingertips. And his all-black tail resembled a licorice whip.

Outside, from where they waited in the hallway, the other cats rattled the door by sticking their paws under the jamb, while the dog nails made staccato scrabblings on the linoleum floor. The kitten ignored them, intent only on Arlene, who had owned, loved, and buried enough cats to know what that look meant.

Like it or not, Arlene had a baby on her hands, a baby who had found himself a new Momma.

Suddenly, the kitten sighed, reached for her hand with one huge-toed white paw, and rested his head against the worn blue toilet tank cover. A smile worked its way onto Arlene's wrinkled face, and stayed there. Patting the kitten's flanks, she whispered, "Why do I get the feeling that there's going to be a lot of jealous animals around the house, hm?"

The kitten blinked his minuscule eyes in reply, and purred louder than ever.

* * * * * * *

Arlene knew from experience never to take an animal in to the vet's office on a Monday; not that she had much *else* to fill her days, but she still hated to waste her time sitting in a noisy office full of yippy-yappy hunting dogs and *poodles* whose nails needed clipping.

She did call the veterinarian office ("Not *another* one," the receptionist had half-joked) to make an appointment for the next day; stool test, full shots, the works. And in between making sure that her other pets were given extra hugs and soft chewy treats, she spent time in the bathroom with the kitten (who had the most indelicate habit of crawling into her lap while she was seated on the toilet; she had to hold him so he wouldn't fall through to the water in the bowl).

The more she looked at him, the *less* offensive his face became to her; by evening he was almost *cute*. The black parts of his fur glistened with delicate rainbow colors, like the wings of a cowbird or blackbird, or the surface of certain black-red petaled flowers. And the *shape* of his face reminded her of something…by that night, when his cries pulled her from her bed, and she had to try to show him—again—how to use a litter pan (her efforts were wasted though, since he let his bladder go on the toilet tank cover, and did the other thing after jumping into the sink), Arlene finally realized what the kitten reminded her of….a tulip. One of those bi-color ones, with the sharp points on the top of the petals, and a narrow base where the flower joined the stem.

After he finally did his duty, and Arlene scooped the b.m. into an old yogurt cup for tomorrow's test, she came back into the bathroom and held the kitten for a few minutes before going back to bed herself.

"Thass all right," she crooned, hugging the scrawny kitten, "Thass all right, you're a good boy." The kitten kneaded her shoulder; there was something odd about the way he did that, but Arlene was too tired to figure it out. She'd have to ask the vet about it tomorrow.

Morning was only a few hours away, and there was scavenging to do.

* * * * * * *

"You know, you ought to set yourself up as an official shelter," the veterinarian joked as she looked in the kitten's huge ears, checking for ear mites. "That one passes inspection, let's see the other one." The vet's dark-rimmed fingers poked in the cavernous depths of the kitten's left ear. Arlene shuddered; she knew that both the vets had to tend to area cows, and horses, which meant that no matter how often they washed their hands their nails were still stained, but dark nails always gave her pause.

"I don't think I could stand working in a shelter. I'd want to keep all the animals," she finally replied, as the young vet began to palpitate the kitten's abdomen. As her fingers worked their way over the fine white and black fur, Dr. Hraber said, "I thought you did that already, Mrs. Campbell."

"Only the ones I find. I don't think I could cope with ones brought in from all over." Talk about abandoned animals made Arlene uneasy, bringing back memories of all the cats and dogs she'd either picked up or had wandered on her porch. Like Guy-Pie, with his rough pads and way of grabbing whole chunks out of the food bowl and running halfway across the room with them before he'd eat. Big gentle Rowdy, her leather collar stripped of its tags and attached name-tag, just an old yellow hunting dog no one wanted on the hunt anymore. Bubba, huddled shivering next to the Coke machine at the Red Owl, chunks of cow manure stuck in his white fur, his ear tips chewed by God knew what, too beat and broken to even let out a *meaow*.

And those were only the animals *she* had found. Arlene had never answered one of those "Free Kittens" or "Puppies to Give Away" ads in the *Ewerton Herald*; for her, looking at them all was wanting to take them all home. True, she worried about people from labs or pit bull breeders coming to take the little animals, but as long as she didn't *see* them, she wouldn't let it pain her overmuch. She had her "children" to look after; if God saw fit to put one within her hearing or seeing, that was the animal she would take in. Just as she picked up cans or went rooting for week-old bread in back of the IGA. There was only so much she could do. Some things, unfortunately, were simply out of her hands.

"—think of a name for him yet?" The vet's question startled her. Arlene pressed her hands against the kitten's pathetic hips, and said, "Haven't given it much thought...nothing much suggests itself, does it?"

Across the white examining table, Dr. Hraber suggested, "Duke? He looks like a Duke's mixture—"

"No, my Don liked John Wayne. The name would make me think of him too much." (Arlene let the doctor assume that she didn't want to think of Don because the memory was painful—as it was, she missed the Duke more than she ever missed Don.)

"Hummm...well, we have to put a name on the vaccination certificate—"

"Silky? His fur is so soft—"

"Sounds good to me. That good with you, huh, Mister?" The vet opened Silky's mouth, and ran a dark-rimmed finger along his gum line. Silky endured the intruding digit patiently. As Arlene watched, she remembered that she had meant to ask the doctor something *else* about the kitten, but couldn't remember it now. Instead, she asked, "What kind of cat do you suppose he is? He's different-looking—"

"What kind?" The doctor waited a beat, then, as she cupped her fingers under Silky's chin, said, "*Ugly.* No, seriously, it looks like there's either Siamese or Oriental Shorthair in there, but I've never seen a cat like him before. I guess something bred with something different and it looked like this. I wish I could've seen his parents. Sometimes different breeds don't cross very well, do they, Silky?"

Silky looked gravely at Dr. Hraber, as if to say, *Please don't make fun of me.* Arlene wasn't the only one to notice that expression, for Dr. Hraber dropped her bantering manner and said, "The stool test should be done in an hour or so. Do you care to wait around or call later?"

Tucking Silky's wedge of a head under her chin, Arlene walked out of the examining room and into the waiting room, saying over her shoulder, "I'd rather call later, if you don't mind."

Outside, after she had paid for the shots, Arlene nuzzled Silky's head and murmured into the cat's sweet-smelling short fur, "Nasty lady said my little boy's ugly...we just won't listen to her, will we? We won't pay the least bit of attention, none at all."

But all the way home, Dr. Hraber's remark niggled at Arlene.

* * * * * * *

The *CAT BREEDS OF THE WORLD* book was written on a junior high level (which is where the book had come from, a discard from the middle school library), but the pictures in it were excellent, so Arlene suffered through the namby-pamby text:

> *...the Oriental Shorthair is a very long, lean cat, with strong muscles. The body is shaped a little like a tube, with extra long hind legs. Some people think its legs look a little bit like a race horse's legs.*
>
> *The Oriental Shorthair's fur can be many different colors, as well as colored in points like its relative the Siamese (see page 59). The fur of this Oriental breed is very short, and fine-textured, like silk.*

(Arlene looked down at the cat curled in her lap and said, "At least your name fits, baby.")

> *Oriental Shorthairs have big green eyes, and even bigger ears. Their faces are triangular and...*

Arlene looked at the picture on the facing page, but there was only a slight similarity between the dark gray cat pictured and the purring kitten on her lap. The Shorthair's whiskers were too long (Silky's were an inch and a half and less), and there was at least an inch or more of space between the ears themselves. Silky's ears all but met in the middle of his head; there wasn't room enough on top for Arlene's little finger to rest. A little over a quarter of an inch at the most. And the

Oriental's eyes were huge, luminous and take-your-breath-away green. Her kitten's eyes were a little bigger than the fingernails on her forefingers, ovals of less than half an inch at the widest point. *Much* less.

The bodies of the two cats were closer, but there were still differences. Silky's hind legs, while longer than the front ones, weren't racehorse-high. And now that she looked at his front paws, Arlene realized what was wrong with them, what had hovered at the back of her mind since the night before. Silky had no claws. He had mottled pink and black pads, and the little fleshy dew-pad on the sides, but no claws.

Sick at heart, thinking that some clod had had Silky declawed then dumped him to fend for himself, Arlene gently flexed one of his paws and turned it around, looking for the telltale sunken incision lines of a declawed cat. Her Beanie, many years ago, had been declawed when her neighbors gave the cat to Arlene before they moved to the Cities. That calico's feet had felt limp around the tips of the toes, where the first joint had been removed along with the nail. And there had been those sunken ugly scars...but Silky's feet were almost perfect. There were the right number of metacarpals under the skin, with no empty places under the skin and fur. He just didn't have front claws. His hind ones were there, needing trimming in fact, but the front paws were free of crescent-shaped nails. Holding the cat's paws dose to her bifocals, Arlene saw that there weren't even any holes where the claws *could* come out.

Letting go of Silky's feet, Arlene said, "Don't worry, your secret's safe *with* me. I won't let that mean old doctor make fun of you, call you a freak. She'd probably call you a mutant, or worse."

But as she sat on the lowered lid in the bathroom, listening to her other pets mill around in the hallway beyond the closed bathroom door, Arlene hugged Silky close as she wondered, *What else might be wrong with him...inside?*

* * * * * * *

Once Silky was free of the roundworms the doctor found in his stool sample, and Arlene was satisfied that he carried no fleas, she let him have the run of her small home. Initially there was a lot of hissing, barking, pissing, and scratching, but within a week Silky had settled in beautifully. Within two weeks the older cats were fighting over whose turn it was to wash his cavernous ears, while the dogs took turns chasing an old wiffle ball around the floor with him.

Silky learned to wait with the others for breakfast, while Arlene combed the streets and alleys, looking for cans and whatever else was there waiting to be found, taken home, and utilized. Once she even found a rubber jingle ball (along with a couple of almost perfect Ekco pizza pans). And July turned into August, which turned into September (which felt like October; Arlene blamed all those space shuttles NASA sent up to foul up the jet stream and ozone layer), and Silky was now one of the family...albeit a slightly lonely member of the family.

The dogs were all over seven years old, and tired quickly, while the next-youngest cat was Guy-Pie, at five years old. At first he had been Silky's "best buddy," but then Arlene noticed how Guy-Pie had trouble swallowing, and even more trouble breathing. *Respiratory infection*, she told herself, and tried to take his temperature, but the tortoise-shell cat bucked and kicked like a bronco horse when she tried to do *that*, so she gave him amoxicillin drops that looked like watered-down Pepto-Bismal and smelled like cherries. (She always kept a bottle of dry amoxicillin powder on hand.)

Guy-Pie took the amoxi without complaint, but he didn't get any better. Putting her ear to his ribcage, Arlene heard a strange hooting and whistling, and said to herself, *Pneumonia…or perhaps pyothorax. They're always fighting over some little thing, nipping ears and tails…maybe someone bit Guy-Pie in the chest and I didn't notice. Guy-Pie has never been a complainer.…*

It wasn't pneumonia, and it wasn't pyothorax. The cat's temperature was normal, but his X-ray wasn't. The other veterinarian, Dr. Mertz, was as gentle with Arlene as if the old woman was his own mother.

"It's a tumor in his upper chest. It's pressing against his heart and thorax. I don't think he's in pain, but I can give him cortisone pills for the duration. Now there's a *slight*, and I do mean very slight chance that it might be an abscess, although I can't find any healed scars on his chest wall. I have this medication, clindamycin hydrochloride—"

Guy-Pie fought this clear, bitter-smelling new medicine, but he didn't cry or complain after Arlene squirted it down his throat twice a day. Once, he did jerk his head, and a drop of the liquid touched Arlene's lips. It was vile, the way paint thinner or ammonia probably tasted. Making herself lick her bitter lips clean, Arlene cried, "Oh, Guy-Pie, I'm so *sorry*...but I have to give it the old college try, don't I? Don't we?" and hugged the trim dark cat with the little upturned nose and big frightened green eyes close to her flannel shirt. And as she cried into Guy-Pie's smooth tan stippled black coat, Silky watched her from where he sat on the counter, small eyes solemn.

And for a month, then two, Guy-Pie ate, still lost weight, kept on taking his pale orange pills, yet never complained, while Arlene forsook her daily Dumpster dives, telling herself that the recycling truck only came every other week anyhow, and that she didn't need to gather as many cans.

The older cats and dogs took turns sleeping next to Guy-Pie; washing his head and ears, purring for him when he could no longer purr for himself. The tumor grew; his chest swelled in either direction. Silky tried to wash his friend into activity, until he realized what was up (or so Arlene let herself believe) and merely slept next to his cobby-bodied friend, waiting.

And when Guy-Pie ate no longer, even after Arlene rubbed the soft smelly food on his ever-paler gums, she wrapped him in a blanket which she held against one shoulder, while she carried the old black gym bag she'd found near the middle school in her free hand.

She couldn't bear to let people see her carrying a dead cat through town on the way home.

* * * * * * *

November wind, sharp and silvery pure as a freshly honed blade, whistled through the little gaps where Arlene's scarf and thin gray hair met. She was walking along the curved spur of tracks near the depot, past the place where Dean Avenue curved out in the opposite direction to the west, scanning the rusted tracks for the right stones. Guy-Pie was a good cat, a beautiful cat. He deserved the finest stones to cover the flattened round of disturbed earth in the backyard. Her pea-coat pockets were heavy and hung low with the rocks she'd already found. Grays, pink-grays, and jagged bits studded with shimmers of mica. (The shine of those stones reminded Arlene of the liquid green light in the back of Guy-Pie's eyes, just before the injection—)

Not worried that a train would run over her (the Soo Line had been sold years before, and the buying company cut out the Ewerton runs), Arlene followed the gentle curve to the west, walking stiff-legged down the middle of the boards, her feet moving in a strange gait as her feet sought out each nearest plank. *Tracks aren't made for walking*, a calm part of her mind thought, as an old image came back to her. Guy-Pie as a kitten, dignified even in his hunger and footsore condition, as he stood on her front porch. Such a pretty kitten, not long and scrawny like most adolescent cats, but perfectly formed and solemn. And how the other kitties had taken to him, with none of that nose-out-of-joint tomfoolery.

("—he's had five good years, Mrs. Campbell, that's the most anyone could've done for him. And remember, he had a recessed testicle when you found him, and if that had remained inside him, he would've been dead in a year from cancer. You gave him years he wouldn't have had. And he was good to your other cats, and that new kitten of yours too—")

And he'd even sat quiet while she plucked off all the fleas that survived his shampoo. Guy-Pie was the best kitty she'd ever had, until Silky came along, at least. And while Silky wasn't like Guy-Pie, not in a lot of ways, he was good in *his* own way.

It had almost done her in when she brought Guy-Pie home, and placed him on the floor, then dragged the other animals over to see him. She had read once that that was important, making sure that the other animals in a household knew that one of their friends was gone. The dogs howled and took off after seeing him, and most of the cats did likewise, except for Silky. He had reached out one white paw to touch Guy-Pie's flank, and when his friend didn't respond, Silky let his head hang down but didn't leave Guy-Pie's side.

Pausing to dry her leaking eyes (*it's the wind, cuts like a razor it does*), Arlene realized that she'd walked well past Dean Avenue, all the way up to the depot. The old rust and cream painted building was abandoned now, with the warped boards showing through fine-grained and silvery in the pale sunlight. On the side facing her were all the old wrought-iron benches bolted to the concrete platform, and above the benches was a multicolored flutter of paper; all sizes, shapes, and shades, attached with thumbtacks, tape, and staples.

After the Soo buyout, people began to treat the old depot like the world's largest message board, putting up layer after layer of paper which grew rust-runneled after a good rain. Shoving her chapped hands into her already full pockets, Arlene stepped across the rusted rail and made her way toward the gravel and stone studded dead grass which lay between the rails and the depot.

Some of the posters were weeks, months old, and wind-worn, while others (written on lined notebook paper, or on patterned recipe cards) were obviously, painfully new:

"Cloths made to order. Any size, any fabick.
You suply the pattern.
Call 555-8743 p.m."

"4-Sail: One (1) used trailor top, like new.
Also almost-new RV, and new child-size RV...."

"To Give to GOOD Home; two Persian kitties,
litter-traned and gentile—"

Arlene had to laugh at the part about the kittens being Christian, even as she mourned the ignorance of the person who wrote the message. There was an address as well as a phone number on the piece of lilac notebook paper, on 7th Avenue East, less than a two—block walk from the depot. For a few seconds, Arlene wavered, torn by her inner misgivings.

On one hand, she had vowed not to take in cats that someone else might want, yet on the other hand, Silky was lonely, and needed a young cat—or cats—to run with.…

Thinking that no one would mind, Arlene tore the piece of paper off the depot wall, and stuffed it in her pockets along with Guy-Pie's rocks.

* * * * * * *

"*I said* will you shut them kids up already?" The young man pushed his long limp blond hair out of his colorless eyes (and past a whey-colored expanse of forehead) as he yelled at his wife in the other room. The shapeless young woman in the thin cotton maternity top only shrugged in reply and shut the door connecting the living room to the sunken back bedroom. The din of the six (seven? surely the young woman had to have been babysitting some of them) children was muffled by the door as the sweatshirted young man went on, "That sign's been on the depot for two weeks now. I was almost set to…*you* know…the kittens." The pale man made a two-handed gesture indicative of something being drowned, forcibly. Arlene nodded dully.

"I told my wife that she's gotta be careful who Mr. Clean mates with, but my wife lets her out into the yard any old time—"

"I take it Mr. Clean is a queen?"

"Huh?"

"A *female* cat," Arlene said succinctly, thinking, *And he claims he's* breeding *cats?* while the young man bent at the waist to scoop Mr. Clean up as the plush red cat sauntered by.

"The kids named her 'fore we sexed her. Name stuck. But she's pure, I got papers somewhere," the man lied glibly, not knowing that no cat is ever issued papers unless it has been sexed. Arlene let his *faux pas* go. She couldn't wait to pick up the kittens, be they pure Persian or not, and get out of this tiny house that smelled like old French fries and stale beer.

Rocking in place on the littered carpet, Arlene asked, "Are the kittens in the house? All my cats live indoors, period."

Nonplussed by her pointed remark, the man pushed a stingy lock of hair behind his ear and said, "They're in the garage. Play in among the old engines and stuff. Course we got rid of the good ones, sold the last of 'em this week. These two aren't for breeding. They're objectionable, y'know. If that makes a difference, I mean."

It was Arlene's turn to be confused. "'Objectionable'? As in—"

The young man led her through the sunken kitchen, out a back door which connected directly to the garage, saying, "Their coloring. It's red, but not the right red. They got tiger stripes on their heads, but no *tiger* markings on their body. Their Ma, she's pure red. Most of the kittens were, 'cept *these* guys." The man scooped up two wiggling balls of fluff crawling near an engine on blocks, and handed them to Arlene.

She let out a soft "Ooooh," and cuddled the kittens under her chin. They were gorgeous, pure Persian as far as she could tell (although one little tail did look a tad too long), with orange eyes and pale orange pug noses. Not quite Peke-faced, but with adorable dips in their noses, and wide flexible white whiskers. They reminded her of those little Troll dolls popular in the 1960s, those pug-ugly dolls with the long manes of odd-colored hair and flat round eyes, only Troll dolls were never this adorable.

"What do I owe you?" she asked as a formality, remembering that she had left her wallet at home. Luckily for her, the man shrugged and said, "Aw, let it go. Saves me the trouble of having to kill 'em. You will have 'em fixed, won't you?"

"Certainly. I believe in prevention," she added, realizing that the jibe would go over his head, but feeling the better for having said it.

After fitting the kittens into her pea coat (her breasts had shrunken from age and disuse), Arlene hurried away from the sorry prefab on 7th Avenue, toward her home to the south. The rocks in her pockets beat against her hips with every step, but it was a good ache.

* * * * * * *

As she expected, Silky and the new kittens (both

males, whom she dubbed Puff and Fluff) got along famously—after a few "I-was-here-*first*" hisses on Silky's part. And as she patted the stones into a rough heart shape over Guy-Pie's grave, she reflected that maybe things just worked out for the best, no matter how painful they seemed initially. One cat died, she went to look for stones for him, and she saved two kittens from death. A minus, but followed by two pluses. She still hurt, but she would heal.

And Silky began to act like a kitten again.

* * * * * * *

Come December, Arlene guessed that Silky had to be going on ten months old, but he just wasn't *growing*. True, his body had no more hollow spots, and sleek muscle had covered the painful bone, but he just wasn't any bigger. Even Puff and Fluff grew; they were close to his size after a month in her house. And it was too cold out to go lugging him to the vet just to have her tell Arlene that she had to expect mutant cats to be different. (Dr. Hraber already called Silky "Bug-Eyes" in honor of his still-bulging eyes.)

Arlene had already held off getting Silky neutered; occasionally he sprayed near his pan, and attacked at least one of the dogs each day, hugging with his big-toed funny paws as he chewed on a big floppy ear, but Arlene kept hoping that he'd get a late growth spurt and fill out properly. Even as she knew in her heart of hearts that he was done growing. He hadn't gained weight since November, and nothing about him had changed since October. (On Halloween some children who came Trick or Treating spied him looking through the window and asked—albeit innocently, "Is that a Spuds Mackenzie cat?")

Once she'd gotten over her fussing and fuming, she had to admit that Silky *did* resemble the tiny-eyed dog in the beer commercials. But she never loved a cat more than Silky, not even beautiful, patient Guy-Pie, Lord rest his soul. Silky was always there, showing up in the oddest places; at her elbow while she rolled pie dough, on her lap when she went to the bathroom, dropping down onto her shoulders from on top the high book-cases flanking the front door, purring all the while.

Puff and Fluff took up some of Silky's time, but not all of it; every night, he curled around her head on the pillow, strange soft paws gently kneading her thin-ning hair. No other cat was allowed on the pillow—on the bed yes, the pillow never—but Silky rested there as if he *belonged* in such a high up, exalted spot. He reached inside her and filled the hollow spot left after Guy-Pie's passing, filled it and then some. Long after he'd chosen her for his Mama, she chose him to be her Best Boy. She still loved the other cats and dogs, in her own way, person to animal. Silky was…different. Not only in looks; she'd long ago gotten used to his looks. In spirit, in *soul*, he was different.

But it wasn't until that January that she learned just how utterly different Silky was from other cats.

* * * * * * *

Arlene was making hamburgers in the kitchen, from meat she'd found and oatmeal, onions and spices she'd bought. Knuckle deep in the gooey reddish mixture, Arlene heard the cats doing *something* in the living room—something noisy enough to hear, but soft enough not to be easily identified—and yelled out, "Cats, you be good, hear? Or no supper tonight!" (She never made good on the threat, but it nonetheless usually worked.)

The noise continued, a puzzling muted wooden *thump* (like someone pounding on a board with a wool-wrapped hammer), then a long silence, then a sound of contact followed by all of the cats running around. Quickly mashing the meat and seasonings together, then placing the bowl of unshaped hamburger in the oven—she knew better than to leave *anything* edible on the counters—Arlene ran her hands under the tap, and flicked off the water from her fingers as she stomped into the living room: She was about to say something, yell something, when she noticed the odd way the cats were sitting around the front door in a wide semi-circle; all facing the two bookcases flanking the door. All the cats...except Silky. Out of the corner of her eye, she caught a blur of white and black; Silky bounding from the floor to the chair by the window to the top of the bookcase between window and door.

The other cats (as well as a couple of the smaller dogs) were watching Silky intently, as if they knew what was to come next. Arlene watched too, as Silky positioned himself on the bookcase, back legs tensed as if he intended to jump onto something higher than the bookcase then wiggled his whipcord body, tensed all over, and leaped into the air—

—and didn't come down on the other bookcase, but kept going *up* in a graceful-beyond-imagining arc, his funny clawless feet spread until the skin was stretched taut between his metacarpals, and his huge, delicate, wind-cupping ears grew large, swelling out like a windbreaker sometimes does in a strong wind, *billowing* out above his tiny wedge of a head like miniature sails—and he was suspended there, in the air, for what had to have been seconds, until he turned his head and changed course to a point between the two bookcases, and still he didn't come rushing down, but *floated*, as easy and gentle and beautiful, oh *God* so beautiful, as a dandelion seed freed by the wind to drift on the invisible currents of the air.

Arlene stood numb, watching as Silky settled gently to the ground on all four feet, making only the slightest amount of noise. Just enough to have been puzzling when heard from afar. Afterward, he and the other cats ran around the room, in sheer excitement over Silky's incredible feat. And Arlene wished that her knees weren't knobby with arthritis; she wished she was small enough to run around in circles with her furry children, and had the right voice to bay out loud and purr and—and—she didn't *know* what.

It was a sight to howl over, to screech and *meaow* and cluck over. No human sound, no human word, could express what she was feeling now. It was joy. It was awe. It was more than her heart could keep inside without exploding like a firecracker suspended in a hot July sky.

She bent down and grabbed Silky; painful knees or not, she and the cat danced around the living room, bouncing with giggles and purrs off the walls, the furniture. It was a *miracle*, as only new, as in brand-new life can be a miracle.

Silky wasn't a mutant, something to be ridiculed, even if he was a *mutation*. He was what the Cat had been striving for through the centuries; a creature of the air, a creature dappled by the sun sliding over its warm fur as it glided with the wind. One with the land, one with the air. Matching the startled birds in their flight. Escaping the ground-bound dog effortlessly. In the back of her mind, Arlene had always wondered who could've been so cruel as to put Silky in that high window...but he was lighter then, with the same huge ears. Suppose he jumped up, hit an air current, and *floated* there?

Holding him away from her body, Arlene now understood Silky's form, its *purpose*. Webbed feet, to buffer the wind. Sail ears, for the obvious reason. Strong legs, for take-off. Super-flat, super-silky fur, for low wind resistance. Few whiskers, so as not to interfere with the airflow. Small eyes, to keep flying dust out.

Just like the birds, she thought, *or the flying squirrels*. Her sudden comparison between cats and squirrels reminded her of another species-to-species comparison someone else had already made.

The Cornish Rex cat, named after the Rex rabbit. She'd seen the picture in her *CAT BREEDS* book....

* * * * * *

When Arlene pulled out the worn book and sat down to read it, the animals and Silky quieted down too. Silky was in her lap as she paged through the book, until she came to the picture of the thin curly-haired brown cat. She scanned the next page, picking out the important facts: "discovered in 1950 by a Cornish rabbit breeder," "Kallibunker was 'backbred' with his own mother, which means that instead of trying to mate him with another bloodline they—" "ten years later another curly-haired cat was found near an abandoned tin mine in Devon, England."

Arlene frowned and backtracked to the part about the "back bred" situation. She didn't like *that*, not at all. When Arlene was a girl, her old cat Mammajamma mated with one of her sons. Papa had had to kill the kittens, during school so little Arlene wouldn't see it. *I wonder how many times they tried this "backbreeding" business?* she asked herself, as Silky gently kneaded her thigh. Arlene paged to the back of the book, to the index, where she found the heading "Spontaneous Genetic Mutations." One of the breeds listed there was the Scottish Fold. According to the text, a kitten named Susie was born in 1961 in Perthshire, central Scotland, at the William and Mary Ross farm. Twenty-one days after Susie and the rest of her litter were born, little Susie's soft ears did a 180 degree flop forward and stayed that way. And a new breed was born.

The Rosses realized what they had in Susie (*did you dance around the barn, making swirls in the straw?*), and began to breed her, even though the British Governing Council of the Cat Fancy refused to acknowledge or license the cat on the grounds that the cat couldn't *possibly* hear, let alone have its ears cleaned properly. The new breed was banned in Britain as a show breed. Nine years later, the United States recognized the Scottish Fold. By that time, standards of perfection ("'*Objectionable?' As in*—?") had been established: small, tightly formed ears. Round head with firm chin and jaw. Short nose and neck. Broad nose, large eyes. Short rounded body. Medium legs and tail. Short coat. Coats of all colors, eyes of blue, gold, or green.

Then came a passage which made Arlene hug Silky closer to her pap-like breasts, and bite her lower lip:

> *...breeding the Scottish Fold is very hard to do. Two fold-eared cats should not be bred together. When they are, the kittens can have tails that are too short, or stiff legs.*
>
> *Another part of Scottish Fold breeding which can be tricky is knowing how long to wait until a true Scottish Fold's ears develop the characteristic 180 degree fold. The breeder has to wait a full three weeks before the....*

Closing the heavy book with a muted *chuff*, Arlene asked aloud, "And after the three weeks are up? What then…the bucket of water in the back yard, or a shoe-box full of babies left for the vet to kill?" A part of her mind told her that she was being melodramatic; *Silly, where do you think they get the straight-ear cats for them to breed with?* But still, what of the kittens who weren't *right*? The ones with the less than round heads, or the long tails and hind legs? What of those objectionable kittens? Surely, the breeders simply couldn't afford to keep the mistakes around, no matter how adorable they might be.

A crinkly ripping sound made Arlene pause in her thoughts, and look down at her feet. Fluff was undoing her running shoe straps, pulling on the long strip of Velcro with his teeth. Fluff was the kitten with the longer tail, the sassy, aggressive one. Arlene wiggled her toes, and both Persians jumped on her feet, hanging on with their short legs. *Cute as the Dickens…but objection-able. It's a rotten, rotten world, isn't it, fellows?*

As if intuiting her thoughts, Silky reached with his left paw to gently caress her chin. The pad was softer than apple blossom petals, and surrounded with a tickly fringe of short fur. Arlene enclosed his paw with her larger hand, giving the paw a light squeeze. Silky blinked his ludicrously, sensibly tiny eyes and rested his wedge head on her chest.

Stroking his velvety ears with her free hand, Arlene said softly, "What's it to be, Silky-love? I can take you to people who know cats, who really breed them. They'd know, they'd understand. Study you, breed you. Give you a fancy name. 'Wisconsin Squirrel Cat' or 'Ewerton Flyer.' You'd be in all the cat books, next to a picture of one of your great-great grandkittens." Silky reached with his other paw to touch her face; Arlene pressed it against her cheek, bending her head low to his. Clear drops of moisture fell on his fur, to roll down slowly.

"But it isn't fair to all the objectionable kittens, is it? And there would be objectionables, Silky, even from a kitty as perfect as you. Happens all the time…and there aren't enough suckers like me running around to take them in. And I do hate waste, I hate to see things go unused, *unappreciated.*" Silky butted his head against hers, as if he understood and agreed. *Maybe he does realize*, Arlene thought, *Maybe, just maybe, he really does....*

When Silky let go of her face and curled up on her legs, Arlene sat stroking his incredible fur for a few seconds, before lifting him off her lap and placing him on Dan's old ottoman. She then walked over to the phone and dialed a number she knew by heart.

* * * * * * *

Arlene timed it just right; she only had to wait outside the vet's office for a few minutes, which she did while standing with her back to the fitful wind. And Silky— wiggling because he was hungry—was wrapped in enough blankets to keep him in-the-womb warm.

When the veterinarian's assistant opened the door at eight o'clock, Arlene shifted the squirming kitten to her other arm as she walked into the half-lit waiting room. Behind her, as the assistant finished turning on the rest of the lights, the woman asked Arlene, "Did you finally decide that Silky had grown enough?"

Arlene uncovered Silky's head; he yawned and blinked kitty kisses at her. "Yes, he hasn't gotten any bigger since October...I guess he's ten months old by now, don't you think?"

The assistant pushed a strand of her black hair out of her eyes, and paused to rub Silky's ears as she made her way behind the reception desk. "He sure doesn't look it, but maybe his momma and father were small cats. Or he might be a—"

Not wanting to hear about the other option, Arlene said, "Poor Silky thinks I'm punishing him...no food or drink since midnight. Had to put him in the bathroom overnight, just to keep him from the other animals' dishes. We didn't like that, did we?" She leaned over to nuzzle Silky's fur with her slightly bulging nose.

"Well, he'll be happier once he's healed. It's hard on an un-neutered male if he doesn't mate—but I shouldn't have to tell you that. You've had a parade of kitties in here over the years—"

Like Guy-Pie. And Bubba. And Puff and Fluff in a few months. But it's different with you, isn't it, Silky? Not just an end to a couple of gonads, is it, boy? But I just won't be around to take in all those objection-ables.... God forgive me, but I won't be.

The assistant reached over the desk to take Silky from Arlene, saying, "C'mon, big boy, let's put you in a nice cage until the doctor comes. Oh, what a good *boy*," she crooned as Silky butted his head under her chin. After Arlene scratched Silky's ears and bent down to kiss one of his extended paws, the assistant headed for the back of the veterinary clinic, saying over her shoulder, "Y'know, Silky's really one in a million. Usually they're either stiff as boards or clawing the walls at this point."

And softly, so softly that the assistant never heard her, Arlene replied, "He really is at that, isn't he?" before she left the office and walked face first into the cutting December wind.

Also in memory of Sassy, Puff and Pumpkin.
Rest in peace, sweet boys…

—A. R. Morlan, 2010

AFTERWORD

Back when I first wrote this novelette, in the 1990s, I'd loosely modeled Arlene on a real older woman in town, one who did have both cats and dogs at home, a widow who Dumpster-dived regularly each day. She and I weren't exactly friends (more like competitors, actually), but I did speak to her once in a while, which is how I found out about her menagerie of pets. Flash forward a couple of decades, and that woman is now gone from the streets of my town, while I'm the middle-aged woman (or something fairly close to her!) I used to see daily. Just as poor, and, aside from pets, pretty much just as alone, too. I just didn't realize that I was writing about my future self.…

A LITTLE PINCH
IS ALL YOU NEED

A sudden and unaccustomed coolness on the top of his head woke Eric, and for a second, he imagined that his feet were cold, too, much colder than they *ought* to be, before he shook off the last of the groggies.

Sufficiently awake now, eyes accustomed to the murky semi-darkness of his bedroom, Eric looked around him and discovered that the troops had deserted their posts; no cats stationed at his head, sides and feet, keeping their commander warm. Hearing the thump of tails against the walls, Eric looked at the windows above the dresser and desk, and saw them—heads and shoulders hidden behind the shades, rear ends exposed and twitching—watching the Rabbit Race out near the backyard compost heap.

"Yo, cats, front and center," Eric mumbled half into his pillow. "The rabbits will be on the lawn tomorrow night. C'mon, guys, I'm cold." He made *mousies under the covers*, drumming the bottom of the bed under the spread and blankets, hoping that the troops would be conned by the delicious rustle of fabric and feetsies. No dice. Not that Eric really blamed the cats; for some reason, the *mousies* weren't in fine form tonight. They weren't very loud, for one thing; maybe his feet had fallen asleep and weren't responding. *Like the rest of you*, his subconscious whispered.

But that's weird, Eric's mind argued, *cuz they never doze off on me unless the cats are curled up on top of them.*

Eric decided to try flexing his feet, get Old Man Circulation going. The hollow sound of the cat's tails thumping against the wall and flat surfaces of the dresser and desk made the fine hairs on Eric's arms and legs stand on end. Feebly trying to drown out the monotonous pounding, Eric pleaded, "C'mon, fellas, keep Poppa warm. Yo! *Cats*! The mousies are gonna escape if you don't stop them from crawling away. Guys, the rabbits will be th—"

His stubbed toe made Eric wince. Felt like a keg of hot nails driven right up under the nail, and the cold floor didn't make the pain any less—

Eric lay still, unable to move, not *daring* to make so much as a tiny, infantile squealing noise, lest it make what he had left anything more than the horrid nightmare it was. His big toe was stubbed; it was throbbing now, and so *cold*, the chill seeping up from the bare floor into the tender sole of his—

Foot, which had no reason to feel cold; it was still in bed, in *his* bed, oh *please* still be in bed. Not outside the covers and on the clammy floor by the dresser *across the room*…which was exactly where it *felt* like it was right now. Leave it to good ole dream logic—We Make

The Illogical Real…like some sort of crazy commercial. He could now make out his legs in the eldritch light of his room; here the twin outlines of his thighs, there the twin peaks of his knees, and then—

—and then he couldn't make out anything else below that point; there just wasn't enough light in the bedroom yet. Nearby, the rhythmic thumps of furry tails meeting hard surfaces matched the steady pounding of his heart. Eric was shivering, so *cold*, like he felt after taking an early morning walk across his dew-covered lawn, the way cool dampness shot straight up through his feet to his—

Oh. My. God. They *were* moving. His feet. *Moving*; one over by the dresser, the other into the hallway, where the runner of cheap carpeting hid the stains on the linoleum, oh, God, *no*, his Foot was inching its merry way along the runner—toes digging into the nap—and into the living room where it stopped, cramped from the unaccustomed exercise. Eric could feel the pain all the way up into his teeth, which began to grind automatically. It was so bad that he almost—but not quite—missed the slight *pinch* as bone and sinew compressed and thinned along the wrist of his right hand. As the cramp in his wandering Foot subsided, Eric slowly brought his arm out from under the covers, just in time to dimly see his wrist become as elongated and thin as a credit card, so brittle that it was only *logical* that the heavy Hand would have to detach itself from his arm like a ripe apple falling from a branch, succumbing to the overwhelming pull of gravity.

Thankfully, there was no real pain in the separation, just a minor tug before the drop. *Not that this is* real, Eric told himself, as his right Hand fell abruptly with a soft thud onto his chest, leaving his pointed-off forearm hovering useless in mid-air. *This is one wild mind-ride, cats, but come morning, you'll get your yummies,* promise, Eric mused. *Tomorrow Poppa's gonna get his act together, not to mention the rest of him, and then maybe he'll tell you guys about this dream—*

After waiting a second to get its bearings, his Hand scuttered across the top of the quilted bedspread, fingernails catching in the loose threads, until it came to the edge of the bed. It paused, while Eric thought, *C'mon, don't just* drop, *climb down the bedspread, dummy.* Which was what it did, alternately clutching and letting go of the fabric until it reached the floor.

Once down, it took off at a fast clip, balanced on fore and middle fingers, just like those *Let Your Fingers Do the Walking* advertisements. Eric had expected it to do the old *Beast with Five Fingers* schtick, inching along on its palm, the way the Beast did on TV when he was a kid (for weeks he had waited for the Hand to come scurrying out from under his bed, ready to choke him like it choked Peter Lorre).

Propping himself up on his left elbow to get a better look at it, he felt the pinch begin in his left wrist (part of a smokeless tobacco commercial popped into his mind, "Just a little pinch is all you need, just a little pinch—").

Ignoring it, Eric looked down at his other Hand.

It seemed so small, so pale, just a wee bit of a thing, really, high-stepping it across the cold floor. Luckily, the cats were engrossed in the antics of the Bugs Bunny cousins outside, so the Hand wasn't in immediate danger of being pounced on and mauled like a catnip filed cat toy. *Not that* my *cats would dare eat* my *hand in* my *dream*, Eric reassured himself, as the left Hand clumsily plopped down onto the hard floor. Unlike its mate, the Left lurched along on its palm, slowly (dream or no, the crash landing *hurt*).

By now, the Right was in the hallway, "walking" toward the living room. The Foot crawled over to greet Eric's ambulatory Hand, while the other Foot, the one with the stubbed toe, inched cautiously over to the night stand, where Eric could see it. The nail on the big toe was beginning to darken, and the top of the ankle was neatly, bloodlessly pinched off.

As he watched the halting progress of the Foot, Eric felt a *twin* pinch—near the hips.

Yo! Unconscious! Dream factory, whatchamacallit, hey! *This is a bit much now*, Eric thought wildly, as the pinch bore down, deeper and deeper, until he could *hear* the bones and blood vessels compressing into a whisper-thinness, *until*—two slight *pulls*, and the Legs began hitching like two arthritic earthworms, alternately drawn up and flattened out, until they were free of his PJ legs. He couldn't reach down to halt their progress with his stump-ended arms. The pinching had begun in his shoulders, too. And the Legs were gone, free, had skeedaddled; a pair of lightly-haired whitish lengths of flesh and bone, thump-thumping along the floor.

Not able to speak now, lest the cats finally pay attention to him—to all of him—Eric's mind raged: *See! You damned dumb cats, see what you did? You left me and now all my parts escaped from the bed! You and you and you and you sitting looking out the windows, see what you all did? Can't even pinch myself awake cuz the Hands got away! There go the Arms! Now who's gonna open up your cat food, huh, guys? You deserters! I hope it happens to you...there! Yeah, cats, lookit that, all* your *tails pinched off...how you like them apples, huh?*

Watching the Cat Tails thump along the floor, followed by his own pinched Parts, Eric didn't notice until too late that the pinching had started in his neck....

* * * * * * *

Eric woke up to a tangled mess of twisted sheets, blankets, hot (whole) cats, and sweaty PJ's. Panting, Eric quickly thrust his arms and legs—with Hands and Feet *attached*, oh thank you, *thank you* God!—out of the covers, and held them up in the air like a baby just discovering his finsies and toesies, wiggling them in the golden morning light. Tears of joy, of pure blessed *relief* ran down his face and trickled in his ears. (He did have a cramp in his big toe, but it was a *happy* ache!)

He felt his neck, checked both shoulders, even lifted the covers and raised the elastic of his waistband. All members present and accounted for, *Sir*!

The troops, all five furry members, sat on the bed, watching Eric's early morning antics with slit-eyed interest. One of them began to lick Eric's hand, relishing the salty taste of his sweaty skin. The cats began to knead and purr in anticipation of breakfast in the kitchen, Eric stroked the nearest cat's head and said, "You guys wouldn't believe the dream I had last—" until the *pinching* of his Tongue was complete, and it fell out onto the covers before he thought to close his mouth.

The cats had breakfast in bed that morning.

AFTERWORD

Remember this one brand of smokeless tobacco which used to have an advertising tag line which read, "A little pinch between the cheek and gum"? That gave me the idea for this. I don't know how *else* to explain it! It's bizarre, even for me....

HUNGER

When David Farley came to New York City, he was a hungry man. In all ways. The job he landed proof-reading junk mail quelled one form of hunger; David was a small man, anyway, and rice, beans and pasta dishes were his forté since college. And being a careful man, conservative in his tastes and habits, he thrived in his poverty, living cheaply, but proudly. One room, hot plate, bath down the hall.

With autumn came the chance to apply for a job at a real magazine; sf fiction, major news stand distribution, subscription base, and paid lunch hours. Proof-reader, and part-part-time assistant to a senior editor. David applied, and another pang of hunger was silenced. But old hunger was stirred: David's scant income was cut by a third. He was demoted from hunger to near-starvation. YMCA, roach motels extra.

Months later, come September, on an afternoon when fall still seemed months, years away, David was hurrying back to work, crossing West 49th at Ninth Avenue, his mind on the miserable toothache throbbing along his left lower jaw, and the fact that he had had to leave the dentist's office with only an appointment he could never afford to keep, when he almost ran into…her.

Her stench hit him first; fulsome, squishy-moist, like toes trapped in too-tight sneakers. Yet, there was a vague feminine odor about her, a sour yeasty tang that made David's mouth fill with bitter saliva. She was coming from the direction of the Port Authority Bus Terminal, but David doubted, instantly, with certainty, that she was one of the homeless who camped out around there, hoping to bum money off tourists in exchange for carrying a suitcase from the inside of the terminal to the sidewalk beyond, or sitting huddled in ratty blankets, like fraying cocoons, in the hard plastic seats within.

The woman—middle aged, old, eternal? David couldn't tell and didn't want to know with any certainty—was too flyblown, too far beyond normal pity or revulsion, for anyone to come near enough to slip her a quarter or let a dollar bill flutter into her cupped palms.

She might have risen from the streets, pulled from the spit and wrapper and ripped movie-ticket encrusted sidewalks like a heat shimmy, to waver and sway in the sun, all but invisible for her natural camoflage, save for her sick redolence, and save for her fluttering nostrils, her liquid hooded eyes.

Slowly, she moved in a curious sliding shuffle, a wind-driven pile of sweat-ribboned scraps and debris, clinging slapdash to her undefinable body. Oblivious to David as an empty Styrofoam cup rolling down the broad ribbon of sidewalk, she inched forward, head twitching and bobbing, heavy under the layers of folded and twisted sweaters encircling her filth-encrusted dreadlocks.

That she was black seemed an afterthought, a mere chance of pigmentation under her patina of grime and dried mucus clinging to the furrows near her nose, her mouth, her heavy-lidded eyes.

Her clawed hands, the fingers twisting in configurations which spoke to David of alien hieroglyphics, shapes whose meaning was unknowable, unclean, framed palms of chalky white-gray: a sick, bloodless color which was scored with broken lines of embedded dirt, a map of the unknown lands from which she had shambled forth into the late summer sun.

Appalled, yet stirred by a numbing hunger to see just a little more, to look fully before looking away, David stood close to the curb, watching the progress of the street person as she oozed across the street (no cars whizzed past her; instead they eased far away from her, as if fearing what contact with her might do to their glossy paint jobs, their glittering radio antennas), her reek a live thing in his nostrils, stinging the tender flesh there, and clawing into his brain, touching soft, dark, shuttered places....

Only, David stood there a second too long. She turned her massive swathed head, only a degree or so to the left, but enough. Eyes like oily marbles, cloudy with only the memory of dark color locked on his rounded blue ones, and in that second of contact without touch, David *saw* her; the tatter of pilled lace adorning one side of the Peter Pan collar on one of the layered blouses she wore, the fresh scab clinging to her bitten lower lip, an orange plastic child's bracelet encircling one greasy wrist, the toes-gone graying sneakers with the tongues lolling across her high-boned insteps.

And, in that second of seeing, came the *feeling* of a hunger deeper than the soul, deeper than eye-pupil-blackness, of hips-knees-shins-toes-souls numb from moving, moving from nowhere to anywhere for ever, of looking for something for so long that remembrance would be of no help when and if the thing arrived in sight…of *wanting*.

The woman's hand made contact with David's bare forearm before he could jerk away, step back onto the safety of the curb, and run down the crack-veined sidewalk. And in the second in which David did slide his arm out from under her twisted hand, David sensed (*knew*) that if he hadn't moved, the woman would have been all over him, pressing her raggy body against his thin, sport-shirt-and-droopy-tie-covered chest, cradling her massive woggling head in the hollow between his head and collarbones, *feeding* off of him.

For the hunger was there, in her gelid eyes and cracked, working lips, and David found himself spinning around so quickly he almost caught his foot on the curb and splayed forward into the sidewalk; almost, but not quite. From the slight elevated safety of the street itself, David stared down at the woman for a second, before walking a block down West 49th until he could lose the woman in the steadily thickening traffic.

David hurried back to work, almost running now, his toothache all but forgotten as bitter saliva swirled in his mouth, like acidic fire he couldn't spit out into the gutter, lest the woman be drawn to the expectoration....

Yet, as he walked briskly, jacket draped over his free arm (his clean arm), he kept scrubbing his forearm, the one she'd touched, against his hip, scrubbing the flesh until fresh sweat made the skin sting, until he could no longer feel the lingering heat of her fingers there, pressing down on his skin.

It was his own fault, for waiting, for gawking...but had she any right to linger by him, when he had no offering of money in his hand, and no lure of fancy clothing or assumed wealth?

Neither of them had had any right in looking, in lingering, yet...the fact that they both had done so niggled at David, as did the persisting sense of want, of need, of *hunger*, he'd felt rising off the woman like steam from something warm, hidden, suddenly exposed to pitiless cold.

And with the persistent memory of her, of her smell, of her unwelcome touch, David felt the reluctant opening of something deep and scarred within him, the flying open of shutters, the splintered wood banging against moldy walls of bitter remembrance....

Before David came to New York, before he finished college, to be exact, his grandmother had gone crazy over the course of one spring and summer. Just what happened to her already-slow mind was hard to say; when people dropped by to try and talk some sense into her, she'd burrow further into her saggy and worn lavender sweater, pull her hairless, shiny, skinny legs close to the legs of her rocker, and let her frazzled mane of stringy brown and gray hair fall over her greasy face before barking, "Mindyerownbusiness!" in that phlegm-clotted voice of hers. Soon, people learned not to stop by and urge her to see a doctor. Soon people quit coming to the house altogether.

And then David's grandmother retreated to her bedroom, off the living room, leaving her door open only wide enough to watch a sharply slanted image of the television set in the opposite corner of the living room. David's family sometimes heard her cough, or sneeze, or snore loudly and moistly, a sloppy fluttering buzz that all but drowned out the television. (Turn up the volume, though, and she'd mumble sing-songed accusations: "Inconsiderate bastards" "Need some *manners* around this *house*" so David's family just began to edge closer to the set, like guilty moths.)

And she *did* things: Broke David's sister's little glass carousel, the one she'd received after appearing in the chorus of the college summer musical of the same name; broke the base of the fragile spun glass bauble, then tried to re-arrange the shattered fragments next to the base, but Susan *knew* what had happened, and bawled out loud before saying in a few choice words when she saw the damage. *That* only brought the old lady out of her room with a shuff-shuff of her frowzy blue slippers and shaking of her plush red bathrobe (and this was in July, hot, sticky, muggy *July*), and with every step the old woman's mouth was working, working, making the turkey wattle under her chin sway and shiver like the last glob of misshapen gelatin in the bowl.

And as this thing that had once been David's grandmother called Susan and the rest of them vipers, bastards, liars and fuckers, David breathed through his mouth; after weeks cooped up in her bedroom (emerging only to sneak food from the kitchen which lay beyond the bathroom which was connected to her room, or to occupy the sole bathroom long enough to cause extreme discomfort for the rest of the family), the old woman *stank*. The smell was worse than the lingering odor she left behind after she finally flushed prior to vacating the bathroom, more cloying than excrement, yet sweeter, too. Like chicken gone slimy, or old perfume soured by sweat.

The old woman had been spending less and less time bathing over the past year or so—self-righteously she claimed that since she never sweated, she couldn't smell bad, even though David's mother had to wash the old woman's clothes separately from those of the rest of the family, because of the greasy-sweet bacon reek her garments gave off—so David should have been used to the smell, but he wasn't.

David's grandmother's hair hung down from under her bandanna in greasy, limp strings, too clotted with dirt to move in the rush of air from the fan in the corner. Idly David wondered what had happened to the woman who'd gone religiously for her permanent every spring and fall when he was a boy. *That* woman was his Gramma. Not this…creature which bellowed in a throaty croak, shaking a yellow-nailed finger at his sobbing sister. Reflexively backing away, David wondered how anyone could have loved the woman in the red robe long enough to help her conceive David's own mother. By the fall of that year, David and his sister were back in school, but his parents moved out of the house which his mother and grandmother co-owned. There the old woman puttered about and half-starved herself, even though their town had Meals on Wheels and Kinship for the elderly.

The old lady alienated every able-bodied man in town who cut lawns, shoveled snow or did any sort of handiwork, until she reached the point where the house was slowly going to rot and David's folks *had* to stop by to bring her food and to arrange for the house to be fixed up. And still the old woman used every opportunity to cut down, criticize, and out-and-out insult everyone with whom she came into contact.

David wouldn't go to visit her—what Susie did was her own fool business—but a few times he grudgingly spoke on the phone with her. Upon hearing that saccharine warble "Gooood*bye*!" he'd slam down the receiver with one hand, and whip her an unseen bird with the other. Sometimes he'd mumble "Bitch" for his own benefit. But still…he couldn't help but feel funny when he opened the card Mom relayed to him from the old lady for his twenty-first birthday. The unsigned card more suitable for a young boy than an adult, with the note written in a shaky, huge hand which was folded around a $100.00 bill:

"Dear David:

May you have the 'Happiest of Birthdays' every day of the year. To me you have been the joy of my life always.

Love,

your Gramma"

The note made David mad and sad and a little bit exasperated. He couldn't forgive the old lady for the way she'd been, even *before* she went out-and-out crazy, but...*yet*...something inside him told David that *he'd* been the rotten one, no matter what names she'd called him when he was a teenager, no matter what she'd done to his graduation pictures (sneaking into his room, into his desk, to grub around in his papers for the pictures of her posed with honors-graduate David—so that she could draw huge blue ball-point-pen goggle eyes over her own shut-against-the-flash-glare thin-lashed eyes), no matter that she'd bemoaned the fact that his parents bought Susie a carnation and rosebud corsage when she graduated high school, saying to whomever was within earshot, "We could have bought a loaf of bread for what that flower cost."

For she was his grandmother, even if she stank,

even if she was a balding, wattled, greasy bloated *whathaveyou* by the time she finally died of ovarian cancer. He'd had to take the word of his family about her bullet-hard bloated belly under the greasy robe, and the other physical changes. He'd refused to come to the funeral, knowing that he'd smell the lingering odor of her flesh over any flowers in the church....

Just as he knew that buying the bouquet of flowers from the vendor near the Museum of Modem Art (he had no appetite for the wares of the hot dog and cold pop vendor also camped out near the broad front steps of the museum) was his way of trying to tell himself it was all right that he'd stopped to gawk at the street person, that he deserved a little something beautiful and sweet smelling and fragile-alive to comfort himself, something to stop the hunger he felt within himself for human contact, for time spent without the need for money to exchange hands—even as the lingering memory of the foul woman's touch burned his skin from within, and a nagging hungry voice whispered within him, *What she was offering you wasn't wrapped around a $100.00 bill....*

David Farley's hunger diminished when he was offered a promotion at his sf magazine after a year of diligent, uncomplaining work. Assistant Editor, a permanent desk, and no more missed appointments at the dentist. Good-bye YMCA, and left-behind roach motels. One room plus kitchenette, and half bath on the lower west side. He no longer walked anywhere near the Port Authority Bus Terminal.

A scant five months later, a second promotion; editorship of a sister publication of his sf magazine, an experimental soft sf/fantasy venture David didn't expect to last six issues, but the money meant good cooked meals at home. Recipes which didn't call for rice, beans, or anything but the fanciest Italian pasta.

The (temporary, he assumed) editor's chair meant that David had suddenly, magically, reached what he considered the inner circle. During the annual party thrown by the parent publishing firm, he was sought out by toadying would-be writers, and treated with some measure of respect by established figures in the genre. Other editors called *him*, and sometimes agents would take him to lunch, sometimes buy him drinks. Nothing cheaper than white wine, nothing consisting mainly of beans.

When an agent for a well-known but recently luckless sf writer (the supposed best-seller wasn't, no matter how well it had amassed votes in the Nebulas) offered to take David to lunch in order to sell David on the un-best selling writer's latest novella, for serialization, David (who had already half-made up his mind to buy the novella anyhow) feigned indecision and accepted the invitation. Anything to escape the ever-growing mound of subs piled on and next to his desk.

The bar near Broadway and Fifth wasn't crowded as David and the agent waited for their drinks, but the man in the cheap tie with the stripes going the wrong way insisted on standing right *next* to David. While the agent was present, playing up his client, the wrong-tie man was easy to ignore, but the agent was wearing one of those clip-on beepers; when a call came through from the agency, the agent downed his Manhattan, bid David a hasty, temporary fare-well and trotted off in search of the nearest pay phone. David smiled slightly over his Tom Collins; the lapels on the agent's plaid jacket didn't line up right. That secret nubbin of superiority David had gained over the agent was sure to mean that he'd get the novella for what he was offering, not what he was being asked to pay.

David was still bent over his drink, waiting for the agent, nursing the last few sips of liquor, when the backwards-tie man spoke up. Shimmering circles of ghosts of the glasses already downed ringed the man's folded hands resting on the bar. In a far corner of the wall, the brackets-mounted TV was tuned to CNN Headline NEWS (stock market listings scrolled across the bottom of the screen, a busy ribbon of blue); the volume was too low to hear, but some report about the on-going shuttle problems at NASA was on. File footage of the *Challenger* appeared; as it mushroomed into white mist and oblivion, then did it again in slow motion, Mr. Wrong-tie said slowly, solemnly, "Know what I was thinking…when it happened? Not *now*, but the first time?" David sipped his drink, not letting on that he could hear anything, least of all the man beside him.

"Was sitting in the living room, watching, and all of a sudden Bill Murray's in my head. In *Stripes*, the scene with the fancy drill work—" Wrong-tie was pantomiming a shouldered rifle, that much David could see out of the comer of his left eye "—an' when they ask Bill where his commander is, Bill, he shouts, *'All blowed up, Sirrrah.'* And Bill, he was in my *head*, all that day, day it blowed up. Just Bill going, *'All blowed up'*—"

David quickly thumbed some bills out of his pocket, left them by the tall sweating glass and vacated the bar (the agent would just have to haul mis-matched lapels over and look for him), Wrong-tie's shouted "Sirrrah!" booming over-loud in his ears.

Outside, Fifth Avenue was almost devoid of pedestrians, so there was really no reason why David should have bumped into anyone, or stepped on any living thing, until....

....the cat wound itself through and around his legs, forcing David to come to an off-balance stop in mid-stride. When he looked down, the cat was still there, a dark smudge against the already darkening sidewalk.

It was just standing there, off to his right, looking up at him with pus-covered green eyes. It was a male; the spreadout face and almost flat nose were unmistakable. Unneutered. And either old or starved enough for it to have a splatter of stiff white hairs in among the flat black fur. The ears were the shape and texture of rotted morrels, almost without points. In fact, the cat's ears were so cauliflowered that there was almost no openings left in them.

The left hind paw was missing from the hock on down. The tail was short, fading away to pencil-thinness. Stiff, broken whiskers jutted out from either side of the mouth, and from the lips hung pendulous rodent ulcers. One fang was broken off close to the gum line, the top of the tooth encrusted with shining, mottled black and brown tartar, like mold gone unchecked on the skin of Brie cheese.

A three-legged cat…wandering around in New York City. David looked around, assuming he'd see a street person nearby, waiting for him to take pity on the animal and offer money to its "owner." Yet another scam, like the black youths and not-so-young men who hung near intersections, waiting for a red light and the chance to swish a filthy rag or squirt fluid from a pump bottle on the windshield of some car, and who wouldn't wipe off the scummy water until they were paid. Fivers or better. Not that David didn't pity those who called cardboard boxes or sheets of newspaper spread over a grate home. He'd lived the borderline life himself, or as close as dammit to borderline. And the hungry animals hauled around by street people may have been company, family, even…but David felt sorrier for the ones who hauled their kids around from shelter to abandoned car to park bench.

But the cat was alone. Ungracefully it sat on rat-furred haunches, staring at David with pigment-spotted green eyes. No one passed either of them for a few seconds. The wind picked up, a cool pressing hand urging him to get back in the bar, or go to his office, or get back *home*, but something about the cat (the very smelly cat—its odor wafted up to him, redolent of old ear wax, dried excrement and whatever else the animal had rubbed against) made David hover over it, numbed mentally and physically.

Perhaps David hovered too long, for without so much as the characteristic wiggle of the rump, the cat sprang up into his arms. Up close, its smell was a living creature in his nostrils, clawing up into his brain, pawing open a forgotten nest of memories. The cat flexed rough-padded paws on his jacket, worn yellowed nails pressing his skin through the double layer of fabric. The thing's mouth was foul; the setting sun glinted off drool-slimed rough lips. And yet, his eyes were so trusting, so utterly, unequivocally *trusting* that David was sure the cat would willingly snuggle into his jacket, hiding silently and gratefully during the subway ride home. David could even feel/hear the thing's stomach rumbling, through his jacket and shirt. But the moment came when David had to either support the furry body with his arms, or let the cat drop.

When the cat hit the pavement, it paused to stare at him—not with reproach, but with that same blind trust and affection. Before David could make up his mind whether to follow it or to briskly walk away, the cat lifted its pathetic rat tail and scooted off, moving surprisingly fast on three feet.

The odor of its paws remained on his jacket, a sharp tangy reek of old pee, cement and vegetation. Park grass, perhaps, or straggler weeds growing up between slabs of broken pavement. Brushing off his jacket, flicking away flecks of something dried and brown and unpleasant, David felt his tongue curl, finally flattening against the roof of his mouth in distaste and something else, something like guilt....

Before David and his sister and Dad and Mom and her mom (not yet crazy, but boy was she getting there) moved from the crappy house on the far outskirts of town, the *dump* with no insulation, no running water, and no sidewalk, that had been all they could afford many lean years ago when they first moved to Ewerton, Wisconsin from downstate Illinois, to the much better house close by downtown, the big white cement-block house with the high ceilings and hardwood floors in most of the rooms, David's family had to get rid of the cats. Not the *indoor* cats, not Diablo and Blackie and Arthur, but Missy (Arthur's mother), and Bandito and Terri, his litter mates. Females, all unspayed ("Not enough, not enough *money*") had already mated with both sisters, producing sickly litters (Terri's kittens had all died), so Grandma's decree went down—the girls were to be banished to the chicken coop in the back yard. They were in heat constantly, some sort of hormonal screw-up (or maybe cancer, David realized years later, after Diablo—also unspayed, but relegated to the back porch of the old house—lived for another eighteen months with mammary cancer, finally dying in his parents' new house, after the hegira from the big white house), and half-wild to boot. So Dad, hoping that they could eventually have the three pretty females fixed, always in that hoped-for *later*, fenced them in, put them in the chicken coop where they lived for a year, maybe more. Living on scraps of food and oatmeal, by Grandma's decree.

David hated thinking about it all, about how brutal life in the country had made them. Like starved creatures themselves, all of them. The hungriest time in his life which David sought to bury deep, deep in his subconscious—a time he almost *did* manage to forget…except for what happened to the cats.

The three cats weren't too bad off in the coop; they were fed, their poop was shoveled out for them, and the snow covered their pee come winter. The walls of the coop were thick and sturdy. (His mom *had* put her foot down when it came to Diablo, the cat he and his sister found out by the sash and door factory two summers before their move. Diablo was delicate, a refined and good cat, and she lived in the house, or out in the back porch when in heat. Grandma bitched, but Mom was getting fed up herself by then.) But when the money Mom and Dad had saved for the new house was finally loosed from Grandma's account, she laid down a last ultimatum, a final jab in her fury about being ousted from the ugly house in the country she'd grown to love. The three indoor cats could stay in the new house. There was a basement for the males. But the "crazy cats," the females who spent their days pumping, endlessly pumping their hindquarters when not eating, Missy, Bandito and Terri (named for the black patch of fur around one eye, like the people in those old Terryington cigarette advertisements) had to *go*. As in…as in on the day after they'd moved into the new house (the day the old lady kicked Diablo just because she was pissed about moving away from "her" home), David and his dad drove out to the old house, bearing a last breakfast of hot oatmeal and milk in a big plaid thermos (it was late February, not *cold-cold* out, but still—) for the girl cats. David watched them slurp up their final treat, until he had to walk away to stand behind the ugly gray house and wait with eyes shut while Dad fired his rifle. Four times. Four times, for three cats.

And in the pick-up on the way to school, the high school set out in the boonies on the other side of town, David half-listened to his Dad say how the cats didn't run away, but waited their turn, trustingly. David didn't ask which one got shot twice, or why she'd been shot twice, as the last warmth of the slain cats seeped into David's feet. Dad had placed the bodies in a plastic sack in David's foot well, prior to driving their bodies out to the dump. Cats there or not, David wasn't about to swing his feet over by Dad.

Years later, when Diablo died, his folks said to hell with the city ordinance against burying pets in the city and laid her to rest outside the living room double window. And planted a rose bush over her that grew middling tall, high enough to reach out and snag you when you least expected it to do so. And no matter how many cats his folks and his sister got later on, David could still hear those four shots. For three cats. But Dad said they didn't run away....

After figuring *Screw the agent, screw the meal,*

David trotted to the nearest subway entrance, but he kept seeing the last image of the black tom cat, the last look he'd gotten before hurrying away from the bar. The cat had only scurried so far, just close to the mouth of a narrow gap between two buildings. Then it stopped, sat down, and *waited* for him. Even after he'd let it drop to the ground. Even after he'd scooted off, bumping into people going the other way. It had looked at him without rancor, waiting patiently for him to return for it. And David didn't stop shaking inside, tongue still protectively jammed against his upper palate, until he was jerking along with the moving subway deep under the ground where the cat was still no doubt standing, waiting for him in pure trust and faithfulness....

When David's magazine folded, not after six but fifteen issues, David went back to doing what he had done before. Assistant Editor at the sf magazine. He was used to the work, and the money was still good. David even managed to move to better digs, three rooms plus bath, not too far from Central Park. He ate at better restaurants, ones which never featured beans or rice in their entrees. He gradually gained some of the weight he'd lost in his physically hungry years, but still got enough exercise to keep himself looking reasonably fit, reasonably hungry, and held onto his savings. The YMCA still had rooms to let.

Then, after some of the stories and novelettes from the last issue of his now-defunct magazine went on to gain berths in the Nebula, Hugo, and World Fantasy ballots, and a story actually won a Hugo (and was rumored to have come in very high in the Nebulas), David's ship came in. A cargo ship, at that. He was offered the editorship of a rival sf magazine, the one whose pages supplied most of the *rest* of the writing award ballots. At one and a half times his old salary. Taxi time. His days of walking past stinking street people (*she* touched *me, with those claw hands*—) and mangy gimpy cats were all but over; when no taxis were available, he knew which routes were free of hooded watery eyes and trusting felines, or nearly so. When necessary, he lowered his eyelids, washing unpleasant scenes in a veil of wavering rainbows and eyelashes. He began to take vacations, far out of the city, where the street people did not dwell and the animal shelters had the time to round up limping strays.

Then, not long after his Christmas vacation in Pennsylvania, David was forced, due to traffic, to drive back into the city through Harlem. The Lincoln Tunnel was jammed with inching cars, and unfortunately the George Washington bridge wasn't too jammed, so David reluctantly drove through Harlem as quickly as traffic and the slippery streets would allow, all the while feeling a nameless dread, a calling of poor to formerly poor that pulled at him like the irresistible force of gravity upon a body falling from a great height to the hard coldness of the pavement below. The rented car was his awning, his shield against the brutal pull of gravity upon his body, his memory, his heart, upon the deep hungering void within him.

David tried to keep his eyes on the ice-encrusted center line, tried not to notice the dull splotches of the people's faces outside the car—the street sitters (more than a few with dogs and scabrous cats in tow, still more with vacant-eyed youngsters), the wanderers, the crazies lashing out at the icy air, the wall-slouchers. He tried not to see the broken windows, the badges of wood and chain-link and tin the buildings wore, their shining surfaces failing to shine much in the white-cold late afternoon light. Newspapers yellowed to the color of dying, jaundiced skin, fluttered a few inches above the ground, too bedraggled to take full, free flight.

David tried to keep *moving*—until the yellow light turned to red too late for him to spurt past the yellow line, and David found himself caught. The heater puffed warm air at him, air that gradually took on a different, worsening smell as the light stubbornly stayed red. David tried to breathe through his mouth, but that only made his mouth taste terrible, like yeasty old underwear and sweaty rags and rancid bacon and ear wax and dried dung and old sour tom-cat-pee and pungent vegetation. With an undercurrent of freshly cooked oatmeal....And still the red light shone, misting slightly in the cold, stretching seconds of agony into minutes of agony. Thinking that a watched light never turned green, David cast his eyes off to his left, looking up, up, *up*—and then, he saw the window.

At least twelve stories up in a fourteen story building. A gray-tan structure, most windows jagged teeth surrounding maws of black within, save for the window near the right hand side of the building's front façade. The one almost near the flat roof, the one with the old air conditioner jammed into the glassless space.

Rags, mostly red plaid against dingy white, were stuffed around the gold-tan air conditioner. A few raw tatters flapped listlessly in the wind, overhanging the window sill outside. What space there was above the air conditioner was filled with some jagged glass, taped in place. And then David saw the swipe of black against the top of the window, a glancing shadow with only the mere suggestion of a form. *But the black shape was cat-sized.*

And only as the light finally flickered back to green did David's mind admit to him, *Someone* lives *up there. In the emptiness, the filth, the cold...*and it could, it just *might* now, have only three legs. And its owner could be layered with Peter Pan collared blouses and rags, and crowned with a turban of old sweaters. For perhaps want had found trust and formed a *home*, not just a dwelling, a squatter's nest, but a *home*.

David found a parking space between a rusted-out Saab and a muffler-less Ford of uncertain make or year. His mind a dizzying rush (*paw gone below the hock eyes like oily marbles Dadfiredfour times wonder who got blasted twice rancid bacon smell on* her *on her clothes "joy of my life always" it waited for me in the alley*), David did remember to lock the rented car—the hub caps were on their own—before hurrying up to the boarded-up front door of the building. Tin under the wood, and a thick chain. With a padlock. No go.

Thankful that the biting cold made the gangs of kids and roaming adults sluggish, huddled near warm steam gratings, David hurried around to the back of the building, squeezing through a bricked alley. The very bricks smelled bad, as if something reeking and maybe even oozing had rubbed against them frequently. And the stubbled, broken cement between the narrow, hovering walls was dotted with mounds of pale, runny cat excrement...and one pile still steamed, pure fragile white steam.

There was no opening to the back of the building, but there was a long fire escape, rusted herringbone stitches against the crumbling fabric of the structure. As he uncertainly ascended the metal ladder, feeling like a dizzy kid climbing his first big slide in the park, David wondered if the street woman had had enough of the bus terminal. Either that, or her stink and her strangeness had long ago become too much for even her fellow cocoon-sitters to tolerate. As the rusty railing left chalky, gritty stains on his soft-gloved hands, David figured that the cat (*it can't be* that *cat, not* all *the way over* here) wouldn't mind a little stink for company, not with its sewer breath and crap-encrusted paws.

The fire escape slats were surprisingly sturdy, the flat rungs clean from frequent use, no doubt. That odor (that horribly familiar odor) clung to the very metal, lingering in the cool air, enough to make his eyes water...but he did remember not to go opening his mouth again. As it was, he'd had to spit a few times over his shoulder to rid his tongue and teeth of the fulsome aftertaste of the car's forced air heat. And as he climbed, pausing at each landing, he ticked off the floor numbers on his cold-stiffened fingers. Starting again on his left hand after the tenth finger was ticked off, his steps grew slow, faltering. Suppose he walked into a crack house? Suppose someone *killed* him? But the worst "suppose" of all stopped him in between the eleventh and twelfth floors, where he stood vulnerable and unshielded on the open metal steps. Suppose the woman and the cat really *were* there…waiting?

Just what he'd do under such a circumstance was something he'd only know by finding out—and then just doing it, period.

When he reached the twelfth floor, the window nearest the fire escape was broken out, all shards of glass carefully removed, no doubt to facilitate easy entrances and exits by someone perhaps swaddled in layer upon layer of filth-stiffened clothes.

As David climbed into the building through the window, his nostrils quivered when his face brushed too close to the wood frame, for her smell had rubbed into the very wood, in the places where the paint was only a colorless memory. But the smell did keep his mind off the fact that he was doing gyrations up over a hundred feet in the air, in Harlem, with only a metal staircase between him and the filth littered alley below. At least no one was in the alley; David could only imagine how idiotic he looked, breaking into a building while wearing a Yuppie uniform of L. L. Bean slacks and down-filled jacket.

In the hallway of the twelfth floor, David had to think hard, trying to remember which windows, and how far in it was, for all the doors in the twilight-dark building (as seen from the street), and it wasn't at the end or the middle but somewhere in between—and as if in answer to his mental question, the third door from the end on his left opened slowly, casting an elongated triangle of light into the hallway. Pale light, weak and wavery as if coming from a flashlight with bad batteries. And the pervasive smell grew stronger, more nose-stinging…yet comforting, too, in the way the odor of food soothed hunger pangs when he was a little boy. It was the street person from 49th and Ninth, not a crack dealer or a pimp with a messed-up brain and a sharp knife—

—at least that was what David hoped, as he walked forward slowly, cautiously. The yellow light was further marred by a strange shape, also elongated, but with a thin upright tail. The appearance of the dark shape was followed with a yowl, not of anger but of feline recognition. Soon the thing was rubbing on his legs, leaving rank hairs on his corduroy slacks, but oddly, David didn't care any more, just didn't give a tinker's damn about getting fur on his pants or cat-paw stink on his jacket. He scooped up the lumpy animal into his arms, hoisted the purring beast on his shoulder (its broken whiskers tickled his ear) and then tentatively knocked on the inside of the open door before entering the street woman's lair.

The bad smell was compounded by expelled human gas, fresh cat pee and some sort of found food that was going bad. Weak dirty light came through the mended top part of the window, and the grill of the air conditioner was a snaggle-toothed dead mouth, jutting into the room where she had made herself a nest: old crumbling newspaper, shed rags, limp vegetable things of uncertain variety, old sneakers, rusty bike parts and green-fuzzed cans.…. And she sat in the middle of that nest turbaned and dreadlocked head even bigger than he remembered it, the furrows near her mouth even deeper and blacker than he remembered them to be.

But her eyes…even without the feeble rays of the battered flashlight stuck in one clawed hand, they would have been *beautiful.* Still oily, still hooded, but… wondrous to David nonetheless. For sheer *wanting*, sheer hungering *need* had to be nothing less than beautiful, transcendent, even.

The cat draped itself on David's shoulder, purring, kneading his flesh through the padded fabric. And although its eyes were flecked with clumps of brownish pigment, half-blinding it, still the trust and love shone through, spreading sun-like warmth across David's cheek. His skin felt almost warm, so dazzling was the trust in the cat's green eyes. It blinked kitty-kisses at him, just like the cats used to do back home. The trust it held in him was that complete…as the woman raised her hands toward David, beckoning him with her hooded oily eyes.

And without thought, hesitation or trepidation,

David moved closer to her, the street person whose odor all but caused the air to shimmer and David's nostrils to collapse in on themselves. When he was less than eight inches from her, close enough to feel her body heat, David knelt down, let those hungering talon-like hands with the horny black rimmed nails rake lovingly against his jacket sleeve, down, down to his gloved hand, and exposed wrist. He did not flinch when she rested her flesh against his, basking in whatever it was she was leeching from him, his being…but he did speak. Softly, so as not to shatter the radiance of this room, this place, this moment. David whispered:

"Grandma, I am so sorry…and girls, Missy, Bandito, Terri, *I am* so *sorry*…but what could I *do*? It was so hard to love—but the hardness didn't make it not so, do you see what I mean? But it wasn't hard for you all to love and trust, even when the craziness made it hard to know what was within you even when I wasn't worth the effort. Even when it was hard for me I ran and ran from where I was, from what I was, but it didn't stop me from hungering, from needing what I couldn't take or ask for…but look. Here I am. I know sorry doesn't make it right, can't change what was wrong…but… well the feeling was *there*, somewhere, in me. *There*, y'know?"

And then the smells and the sorry sights blurred away from him, runny and watery as rain, as strange fluid squirted on a windshield. And later, he remembered the touch, on his sleeve, his face, the back of his neck, but the fingers and paws were all wrong—yet right, too. The fingers were too much like those he'd remembered from the time before his Gramma went crazy-mean. And the small paws were too soft, too numerous by far....But not wanting to shatter the precious thing given to him after long years of needing, of hurting, of hungering for forgiveness, he kept his eyes shut as he backed out of that stinking place, only opening them when he reached the hallway.

Then he ran, not daring to look back, to *confirm*, until he reached the window exit and barreled down the ringing metal steps, his breath a faint hazy plume behind him. When he reached the dark alley, he paused for a ragged breath; then, when his breathing was normal, he made his way back to the street where he saw in the frosty glare of the streetlight that his hub-caps, antenna and windshield wipers were gone, but the sight of his denuded car only made David smile. He hoped that whatever money whoever took the parts had gotten would go a little way toward stopping whatever hunger had driven the person to thievery in the first place. It didn't matter to him which altar the person prayed before, seeking release from their private hunger and want.

It didn't matter to David at all, as he climbed behind the wheel, and headed for his apartment, not even stopping on the way home for something to eat. He was quite full, for the first and final time.

AUTHOR'S NOTE

Inspired by the non-fiction of Alan Rodgers, this work is nonetheless 90% autobiographical. In memory of Missy, Bandito, Terri, Blackie, Diablo, Arthur, and Rocky I. And Spooky and Thelma, too.

AFTERWORD

As the author's note states, 90% of this is real/very slightly altered—while I was/am an only child (thus, the horrible things which happened in this piece happened only to me, not an imaginary sister), and didn't have my father around when I was younger (thanks to my mother and her demented sick pervert of a mother kidnapping me when I was small and whisking me half a continent away in 1961), almost everything which happens to David Farley happened to me...save for 90% of the New York part. Some of the early sections of this story were based on a Foreword in a *Night Cry* magazine issue which I admired, and while I got permission from the editor to quote parts of it in the first few pages of this story, he declined to allow me to add his name to the byline of the finished piece, instead saying I could just "take" his short non-fiction sketch about his encounter with a homeless woman for the purposes of my story (which he also declined to buy for the magazine).

The three-legged cat was real; while he lived in Wisconsin, and was part of my life for a short time (until my mother—who wasn't all that stable herself since the time she'd given birth to me, and who is even worse shape now—tossed him out of the house for spraying the front door; he tried to come back in, but she wouldn't allow it, so I made a home in a box for him by the back door, until he finally just vanished... but not until he'd impregnated a neighbor's cat [whom I eventually got when they got tired of her having kittens all the time; her name was Princess], and I ended up with three of *those* kittens, Rocky, Apollo, and Bruiser)—but I cannot forget him. His plight is seared on my mind, as is that of the three females who died such a senseless and pitiful death out in the country outskirts of my town. I only wish the family friend who did the deed had turned his rifle on that disgusting skank who'd ordered the execution of those innocent animals. She died a death which was much too easy in 1999—as it was, I wish I had never written this story, since the ending is all wrong. No way now would I ever feel compelled to say I was sorry for anything I did or said to that evil creature who bore my mother. To me, she was lower than the lowest form of life on Earth....

To this day, I cannot be around freshly cooked oatmeal, or even look at a mere picture of a chicken coop, without feeling physically ill, sick to my very soul....

WHITE COMMA

White comma against
heat-stick asphalt,
her head curled close to her
limp, brown-gray flecked tail,
the heat of her body
mirrors the street warmth below

So much so
that I carry her most
carefully, tenderly,
for block
after block,
taking her to the home
she never lived to see

And on the ersatz grassy green
of my front porch floor
I cradle her in
old sheets meant for
keeping the plants warm against
the frost
making sure her sightless
eyes and breathless

nose are exposed to the air
she doesn't need

For all the hours she
rests there, beyond the need for comfort
I watch her from the porch window,
telling myself that the wind
will soon stop blowing,
and that she'll make the sheet above her rise
on its own soon

White comma against
peeling green-painted boards,
crossed paws pointing
forward, forward
toward the porch wall,
cool body mirroring the wood's
dead lack of warmth

The hole by the garage
has been dug,
the crumbling soil
patted smooth,
pressed smooth,
she was still-kitten small
she was comma still
on an unfluttering page.

AFTERWORD

Little comment here; I did find a dead kitten, still quite warm, on the street one day, and took it home—but first left it on the front porch, lying in a towel, and kept looking at it, waiting, hoping, that maybe, just maybe it wasn't dead, but just hurt. Eventually, I buried her by my garage. She *was* really dead.

NO HEAVEN WILL NOT
EVER HEAVEN BE...

There are no ordinary cats.

—Colette

Not too long ago, it wasn't too uncommon for someone driving down Little Egypt way, where southern
Illinois merges into Kentucky close to the Cumberland
River, to see oh, maybe five-six Katz's Chewing Tobacco barn advertisement within a three-or four-hour
drive; in his prime, Hobart Gurney was a busy man.
Now, if a person wants to see Gurney's handiwork,
they have to drive or fly out to New York City, or—if
they're lucky—catch one of the traveling exhibitions
of his work. *If* the exhibitors can get insurance—after all, Gurney was sort of the Jackson Pollock of the
barn-art world; he worked with what paints he had,
with an eye toward getting the job done fast and getting his pay even quicker once he was finished, so
those cut-out chunks of barn wall need to be babied
like they were fashioned out of spun sugar and spider
webs—and not just flaking paint on sometimes-rotting
planks. Someone once told me that the surviving

Katz's barn signs had to be treated with the same sort of preservation methods as the relics unearthed from Egyptian tombs—now *that* would've tickled old Hobart Gurney's fancy, as he might've put it.

Oh, not so much the preservation part, but the Egyptian aspect of it all, for Gurney did far more than paint Katz's Chewing Tobacco signs for a living (not to mention for a good part of his life, period); he *lived* for his "Katz's cats"

Died for them, too. But that's another story…one you won't read about in any of those books filled with photographs of Gurney's barn signs, or hear about on those PBS or Arts & Entertainment specials on his life and work. But the story rivals any ever told about the cat-worshiping Egyptians…especially since Hobart knew his cats weren't gods but love them anyhow. And because they loved *him* back.…

* * * * * * *

When I first met Hobart Gurney, I thought he was just another one of those old men you see in just about every small town in the rural heartland; you've seen them—old men of less than average height, wearing pants that are too big in the waist and too long in the leg, held up by suspenders or belts snugged up so right they can hardly breathe, with spines like shallow C's and shoulders pinched protectively around their collarbones, the kind of old men who wear too-clean baseball caps or maybe tam-o-shanters topped with fluffy pom-poms, and no matter how often they shave, they always seem to have an eighth-of-an-inch-long near-transparent stubble dusting their parchment cheeks. The kind who shuffle and pause near curbs, then stop and stand there, lost in thought, once they step off the curb. The kind of old man who's all but invisible until he hawks phlegm on the sidewalk, not out of spite, but because men *did* that sort of thing without thinking years ago.

I was adjusting the shutter speed on my camera when I heard him hawk and spit not two feet away from me—making that irritating noise that totally blows one's concentration. And it was one of those days when the clouds kept moving in front of the sun every few seconds, totally changing the amount of available natural light hitting the side of the barn whose painted side I was trying to capture...without thinking, I looked back over my shoulder and grumped, "You *mind*? I'm trying to adjust my camera—"

The old man just stood there, hands shoved past the wrists into his trouser pockets, a fine dark dribble of tobacco spittle still clinging to the side of his stubbled chin, staring mildly at me with hat-bill-shaded pale-blue eyes. After a few false fluttering starts of his chapped-lipped mouth, he said, "No self-respectin' cat ever wants to be a model...you have to sorta sneak up on 'em, when they ain't payin' *you* no mind."

"Uh-huh," I said, turning my attention back to the six-foot-tall cat painted next to the neatly-lettered legend: KATZ'S CHEWING TOBACCO—IT'S THE KATZ'S MEOW. This Katz's cat was one of the finest

I'd seen yet—unlike other cat-logo signs, like the Chessie railroad cat, for instance, every Katz's cat was different; different color, different pose, sometimes even more than one cat per barn sign. And this one was a masterpiece; a gray tiger, the kind of animal whose fur you *knew* would be soft to the touch, with each multi-hued hair tipped with just enough white to give the whole cat an aura-like sheen, and a softly-thick neck that told the world that this cat was an unneutered male, old enough to have sired a few litters of kittens but not old enough to be piss-mean or battle-scared. A young male, maybe two- or three-years-old. And his eyes were gentle, too; trusting eyes, of hazy green touched with a hint of yellow along the oval pupils, over a grayish-pink nose and a mouth covering barely visible fang tips. He was resting on his side, so all four of his paw pads were visible, each one colored that between gray and pink color that's a bit of each yet something not at all on the artist's color wheel. And his *ombré*-ringed tail was curled up and over his hind feet, resting in a relaxed curl over his hind paws. But something in his sweet face told a person tht this cat would jump right up into your arms if you only patted your chest and said "Come 'ere—"

But...considering that this cat was mostly gray, and the barn behind him was weathering fast, I had to make sure the shutter speed was adjusted *so*, or I'd never capture this particular Katz's cat. Not the way the clouds were rolling in fast and faster—

"Don't look like Fella wants his picture took today,"

the tobacco-spitting old man said helpfully, as I missed yet another split-second-of-sun opportunity to capture the likeness of the reclining cat. That did it. Letting my camera flop down against my chest by the strap, I turned around and asked, "Do you own this barn? Am I supposed to pay you for taking a picture or what?"

The old man looked at me meekly, his bill-shaded eyes wide with hurt as he said around a glob of chaw, "I already got my pay for that 'un, but I s'pose you could say it's my *cat*—"

When he said that, all my irritation and impatience melted into a soggy feeling of shame mingled with heart-thumping awe—this baggy-trousered old man had to be Hobart Gurney, the sign painter responsible for all of the Katz's Tobacco signs dotting barns throughout southern Illinois and western Kentucky, the man who was still painting such signs up until a couple of years ago, stopping only when old age made it difficult for him to get up and down the ladders.

I'd seen that profile about him on CNN a few years ago, when he was painting his last or next-to-last Katz's sign, but most old men tend to look alike, especially when decked out in the ubiquitous uniform of a baseball cap and paint-splattered overalls, and at any rate, the work had impressed me more than the man who created it....

Putting out my hand, I said, "Hey, sorry about what I said...I—I didn't mean it like that; it's just that I only have so many days of vacation left, and the weather hasn't exactly been cooperative—"

Gurney's hand was dry and firm; he shook hands until I had to withdraw my aching hand, as he replied, "No offense meant, no offense taken. I 'spect Fella will wait awhiles until the clouds see fit to cooperate with you. He's a patient one, is Fella, but shy 'round strangers." The way he said "Fella," I knew the name should be capitalized, instead of it being a generic nomenclature for the animal at hand.

Judging from the way the clouds scudded across the sun, I figured that Fella was in for a good long wait, so I motioned to the rental car parked a few yards away from the barn, inviting Gurney to share one of the cans of Pepsi in my backseat cooler. Gurney's trousers made a raspy rubbing noise when he walked, not unlike the sound a cat's tongue makes when it licks your bare arm. And when he was speaking in close quarters, his tobacco-laced breath was sort of cat fetid, too, all wild-smelling and warm. The old man positioned himself half in and half out of my car, so he could see his Fella clearly, while still keeping his body in the relative warmth of my car. Between noisy slurps of soda, he told me, "Like I said, no self-respectin' cat aims to model for you, so's the only way to get around it is to make your *own* cat. Memory's the best model they is—"

I almost choked on my Pepsi when he said that; all along, I'd assumed that Gurney had used whatever barn cats were wandering around him for his inspiration...but to create such accurate, personable cats from memory and imagination—

"Funny thing is, when I was hired on to work for Katz, back in the thirties, all they was interested in was getting' their name out in front of the public, in as big letters as possible. That I added the cats to the Katz's signs was my idea—didn't get paid no extra for doin' it, neither, But it seemed natural, you see? And it did get folks' attention. 'Sides, them cats, they kept me company, while I was workin'—gets mighty lonely up on that ladder, with the wind snaking down your shirt collar and no one to talk to up that high. Was sorta like when I was a boy, muckin' out my pa's barn, and the barn cats, they'd come snaking 'round my legs purrin' and sometimes jumpin' straight up onto my shoulders, so they'd hitch a free ride while I was workin'—only I didn't get 'round to givin' too many of them cat's names, you see, 'cause they was always comin' or goin', or getting' cow-crushed—oh, them cows didn't mean no harm, see, it's just they was so big and them cats too small when they'd try snuggling up wi'em on cold winter nights. But I sure did enjoy their company. Now you may laugh at this, but—" Here Gurney lowered his voice, even though there was no one else around to hear him but me and the huge painted Fella resting on the side of the abandoned barn. "—when I was a young'un, and even a *not* so young'un, I had me this dream. I wanted to be small, like a cat, for oh, maybe a night or so, just long enough for me to snuggle down with a whole litterful of cats, four-five of 'em, all of us same-sied and warm in the hay, and we'd tangle our legs and whatnot in a warm pile, and they'd lick my face and then burrow their heads under my chin, mine under theirs, and we'd sleep for a time. Nothing better for the insomnia than to rest with a cat purring in your ears. 'Tis true. Don't need none of them sleepin' pills when you gots yourself a cat.

"That's why I took the Katz's Tobacco job when I heard of it, even though I wasn't too keen on heights. 'Course, it bein' the Depression was a powerful motivator, too, but the *name* Katz was just too good to pass by...and them not minding when I dickied with their adverts was heaven-made for me, too. Struck me funny, when them television-fellers interviewed me and all, when I was paintin' the little girls—"

Gurney's words made me remember the album of Katz's signs I kept locked in the trunk of the car (not my only set, but a spare album I used for reference, especially when coming across a barn I may have photographed before, under different lighting or seasonal circumstances); too excited to speak, I got out of the backseat and hurried for the trunk, while Gurney kept on talking about the "pup reporter" who'd interviewed him for that three-minute interview.

"—and he didn't even ask me what the cats' names was, like it didn't matter none to—"

"Were these the 'little girls'?" I asked as I flipped through the album pages until I found the dry-mounted snapshot of one of the most elaborate Katz's signs: four kittens snuggled together in a hollowed-out bed of straw, their pointed little faces curious yet subtly wary, as if they'd all burrow into the straw if you took one step closer to them. Clearly a litter of barn kittens, even if you discounted the straw bedding; these weren't Christmas-card-and-yarn-balls kittens, cavorting like live Dakin kittens for a Madison avenue artist, but feral-type kittens, the kind you'd be lucky to coax close enough to sniff your fingers before they'd run off to hide in the farthest corners of the manure-scented barn where they were born. The kind of kitten who'd grow up slat-thin and long-tailed, slinking as if sizing up whether or not to take a sharp-clawed swipe at your shoe before running for cover. The kind of cat you know will get kittened-out before she's three-years-old, winding up saggy-bellied and defensive by the time she's four.

But when Gurney saw the eight-by-ten enlargement, his face lit up and his puckered lips stretched out into a broad grin, exposing what my own grandfather used to call "dime-store choppers" of an astonishing Chiclets gum uniform squareness and off-whiteness.

"You took a picture of my little girls! Usually they're tricky ones, on 'count of Prissy and Mish-Mish lookin' so much alike, but you caught 'em, by gummy, got 'em in just the right light—"

"Wait, wait, let me get this down," I said, reaching over the seat for the notebook and pen resting on the front passenger seat. "Now, which one is which?"

His face glowing with the kind of pride most men his age took in showing off pictures of their grand-children (or even great-grandkids), Gurney pointed at each kitten in turn, stroking their chemically-captured images with a tender, affectionate forefinger, as if chucking each under her painted chin. "This 'un's Smokey, the tiger gray, and here's Prissy—see how dainty she looks, with them fox-narrow eyes and little points on her ears?—and right next to her is Mish-Mish, even though they're both calicos, Mishy's a little more patchy-colored than usual—"

"'Mish-Mish'?" I asked, not knowing how he'd come up with that name; Gurney's answer surprised—and touched—me.

"Got that name from the *Milwaukee Journal* Green Sheet, where they put all their funnies and little offbeat articles...was an article about the Middle East, and it mentioned how them A-rabs like cats so much, and how their version of 'Kitty-kitty' was 'Mish-Mish,' which is their lingo for peach color, on 'count of most of their strays bein' sorta peachy-orange. See how Mish-Mish's face is got that big splotch of peach on it? Oh, I know we're not s'posed to care what them A-rab folks think, on 'count of them bein' the enemy or whatnot, but you can't fault a people who care so much for their cats too much. Heard tell the Egyptians worshipped their cats, like gods...done up their pets as mummies, the whole shebang. So's I don't even mind when their descendants says they hate us, long as they take care of their cats—'cause a man who can hate a cat can't much like hisself, *I* says."

I had to laugh at that; before gurney could go on, I quoted Mark Twain from memory: "If man could be crossed with the cat, it would improve the man but deteriorate the cat—"

Now it was Gurney's turn to laugh, until he spittle-flecked his shirt collar before he went on. "Anyhows, next to Mish-Mish is Tinker, only you can't tell from lookin' at her that she's a girl, on 'count of her only bein' two colors and all, but from personal experience, most gray cats with white feet I've seen's been girls. Don't know why that is…sorta like how you never see a white cat with black feet and chest, like you see black cats with white socks and bibs. Funny how nature works that way, ain't it?"

Having told me the names of the "little girls" (which I dutifully wrote down in my notebook), Gurney began paging through the rest of the album, matching heretofore anonymous painted felines with the names that somehow made them real—at least to the man who created them: black-bodied and white-socked Ming, with his clear, clear green eyes and luxurious long fur with a couple of mats along the chest; calico beanie with her rounded gray chin and owl-like yellow-green eyes; dandelion-fuzzy Stan and Ollie, black-and-white tuxedo-patterned kittens, one obviously fatter, but both still too wobbly-limbed and tiny-eared to look anything but pick-me-up adorable; and too many more to remember offhand (thank goodness I had many clean pages left in my notebook that afternoon). But once each cat was named, I could never again look at it as just another Katz's Tobacco cat; for instance, knowing that Beanie was *Beanie* made her *into* a cat, one with a history and a personality…you just knew that she was full of beans when she was a kitten, getting into things, playing with her tail until she'd spun herself like a dime-store top....And for a moment, Gurney's cats became more than pigment and imagination. Not unlike the work of regular canvas-easels-and-palette artists, or those natural-born billboard painters, the legendary ones who never needed to use those grid-like blueprints to create the advertisements.

It was sad, really, how that reporter had missed out on the essence of Gurney's work; all the "pup reporter" seemed to be interested in was how *long* Gurney had been at it.

As Gurney looked at the last of the barn pictures I'd taken and enlarged, he said shyly, "I feel sorta humbled by this and all...it's like I was one of them art-fart painter guys, in a gallery 'stead of a regular workin' Joe...Oh, not that I'm not pleased...it's just... oh, I dunno. It just seems funny to have my cats all put in a book form, 'stead of them just *bein'* out where they are, in the open and all. Like they was suddenly domesticated 'stead of bein' regular barn kitties."

I didn't know how to answer that; I realized that Gurney must be astute enough to realize that his signs *were* works of art—he may have been slightly inartic-ulate, and most likely unschooled, but he wasn't igno-rant by any means—he was obviously in a quandary; on the one hand, he was from a time when work was simply something you got paid for, period; yet on the other hand, the fact that he'd been interviewed on TV and caught me taking pictures of his efforts must have been an indication that his work *was* something special. He couldn't quite cope with having a fuss being made over something he'd considered to be paid labor.

I gently lifted the book off his lap and placed it on the seat between us before saying, "I can empathize with you there…I work as an advertising photographer, taking pictures of products for clients, and when someone praises me for my composition, or whatever, it can be a strange feeling…especially since I'm just a go-between when it comes to the product and the consumer—"

Gurney's water pale-blue eyes were darting around as I spoke, and for a moment I was afraid that I was losing his attention, but instead he surprised me by saying, "I think Fella's lost his shyness…the sun's been shining for a good minute now."

Quickly I got out of the car and positioned myself in front of the barn; true to Gurney's word, Fella was no longer shy, but exposed in all his sunlit perfection against the sun-weathered barn. It's funny, but even though the lettering next to the cat was badly flaked, I could almost see every individual hair of the tomcat's fur.

And behind me, Hobart Gurney took a noisy slurp of soda as he repeated, in the way of old men you find in every small town, "Yessirree, my Fella's not shy anymore…."

* * * * * * *

I said goodbye to Gurney a couple of hours later,

outside the adult day-care center and seniors apartment where he lived; without going in, I knew what his room must be like—single bed, with a worn ripcord bedspread, some issues of *Reader's Digest* large-print edition on the bed-stand, and a doorless closet filled with not too many clothes hanging from those crochet-covered hangers, and—most depressing of all—no animals at all to keep him company. It was the sort of place where they only bring in some puppies or kittens when the local newspaper editor wants a set of human-interest pictures for the inner spread during a dull news week—"Oldsters with Animals" on their afghan-covered laps.

Not the sort of place where suddenly-small men snuggle with litters of barn cats in a bed of straw.

With an almost comic formality, Gurney thanked me for the Pepsi and for "letting me see the kitties" in my album. I asked him if he got out much, to see the signs in person, but instantly regretted my words when he nonchalantly spit at his feet before saying, "Don't get 'round much since I turned in my driver's license... my hands aren't as steady as they used to be, be it with a brush or with a steering wheel. Once I almost run over a cat crossing a back road and tol' myself, 'This is it, Hobart' even though the cat, she got away okay. Wasn't worth the risk...."

Not knowing what else to do, I opened the back door of the car and brought out the album; Gurney didn't want to take it at first, even though I assured him that I had another set of prints plus the negatives back in my studio in New York City. The way he brushed the outside of the album with his fingers, as if the imitation leather was soft tiger-stripe fur, was almost too much for me; knowing that I couldn't stay, couldn't see any more of this, I bid him farewell and left him standing in front of the oldsters' home, album of kitties in his hands. I know I should've done more, but what could I do? Really? I'd given him back his cats; I couldn't give him back his old life…and what he'd shared with me already hurt too much, especially his revelation of the smallness fantasy. I mean, how often do even people who are close to each other, like old friends, or family, reveal such intimate, deeply *needing* things like that— especially without being asked to? Once you know things like that about a person, it gets a little hard to face them without feeling like you have a bought-from-a-comic-book-ad pair of X-ray glasses capable of peering into their soul. Nobody should be that vulnerable to another living being.

Especially one they hardly know.…

* * * * * * *

A few days after I met Hobart Gurney my vacation in the Midwest was over, and I returned to my studio, to turn lifeless sample products into…something potentially essential to people who didn't know they needed that thing until that month's issue of *Vanity Fair* or *Cosmopolitan* arrived in the mail, and they finally got around to paging through the magazine after getting home from work. Not that I felt responsible for turning the unknown *into* the essential; even when I got to keep what I photographed, it didn't mean squat to me. I could appreciate my work, respect my better efforts… but I never gave a pet name to a bottle of men's cologne, if you get my drift. And I envied Hobart for being able to love what he did, because he had the freedom to *do* it the way he wanted to. And because the now-defunct Katz's Chewing Tobacco people could've cared less what he painted next to their logo. (Oh, for such benign indifference when it came to *my* work!)

But I also pitied Hobart, because letting go of what you've come to love is a hard, hard thing, which makes the ending of that creative, *loving* process all the harder to take, especially when the ending is an involuntary thing. What had the old man said in the TV interview? That he was too old to climb the ladder anymore? That had to have been as bad as him realizing that he couldn't drive safely anymore.…

And the funny thing was, I got the feeling that if he could have climbed those ladders, he would've still been putting those man-sized cats on barns, whether Katz's paid him or not.

I honestly couldn't say the same about what *I* did for a living.

* * * * * * *

I was in the middle of shooting a series of pictures of a new women's cologne, which happened to come in a bottle that resembled a piece of industrial flotsam more than a container for a fragrance boasting "top notes of green, with cinnamon undercurrents"—whatever *that* meant, since the stuff smelled like dimestore deodorant, when my studio phone rang. I had the answering machine on Call Screening, so I could hear it while not missing out on my next shot...but I hurried to the phone when a tentative-sounding voice asked, "Uhm...are you the one who dropped Mr. Gurney off at the home a couple of months ago?"

"Yeah, you're speaking to me, not the machine—"

The woman on the other end began without preamble, "Sorry to bother you, but we found your card in Mr. Gurney's room...the last anyone saw of him he was carrying that album you give him under his arm, before he went for his walk, only he never went for a walk for a week before—"

The sick feeling began in my stomach and soon fanned out all over my body; as the woman in charge of the old people's home rambled on, telling me that no one in the area had seen the old man after he'd accepted a lift from someone with Canadian plates on his car, which naturally meant that he could be anywhere, but maybe headed for New York. I shook my head, even though the woman couldn't possibly see me, as I cut in "No, ma'am, don't even try looking here. He's not far away...I'm sure of it. If he's not still in Little Egypt, he's across the border in Kentucky...just look for the Katz's Tobacco signs—"

"The what?"

I pressed the receiver against my chest, muttered *You stupid old biddy* just to make myself feel better, then told her, "He painted signs, on barns…he's saying goodbye to the signs," and as I said the last few words, I wondered at my own choice of words…even as my own artist's instincts—instincts Gurney and I shared—told me that I had, indeed, chosen my words correctly.

* * * * * * *

Despite the fact that the woman from the rest home had gotten her information from me, she never bothered to call me back when Hobart Gurney's body was found, half buried in the unmown grass surrounding one of the abandoned barns bearing his loving handiwork; I found out about his death along with all the other people watching CNN that late-fall evening— the network reran the piece about his last or next-to-last sign-painting job, along with an oddly sentimental obituary that ended with a close-up of the "little girls," whose particular sign the old man's body had been found under. The camera zoomed in for a close-up of Mish-Mish, with her patchwork face of mixed tan and gray and white, with that peach-colored blotch over one eye, and she looked so poignant yet so *real* that no one watching—be they cat lover or not—could fail to realize what may've been more difficult to realize during that warts-and-all initial CNN interview, which plainly showed how unsophisticated and gauche Hobart Gurney may have seemed to be on the outside (so much so, perhaps, that it made underestimating his works all the easier); that Gurney was more than a great artist: He was a genius, easily on the par of Grandma Moses or anyone of her ilk.

J. C. Suares was the first person to put out a book devoted to Katz's Cats, as Gurney's creations were to become popularly known. Many famous photographers, including Herb Ritts, Annie Leibovitz, and Avedon, took part in that collection; I wasn't one of them, but I did get in on that other collection put together for one of the AIDS charities. Then came the specials on what Gurney would've called the "art-fart" stations, and there's even been word of a postage stamp bearing his likeness, along with one of the Katz's Cats.

The irony was, I seriously doubt Gurney would've truly enjoyed all the fuss made about his work; what he'd created was too private for all *that*. Not when he'd so lovingly stroked the images of his "little girls" faces in that rental car of mine, and not when he'd so spontaneously shared that cat-size dream of his from his barn-mucking boyhood so many years—and barn cats—ago. But at least for me, there was one benefit from his life, and his work, becoming so public. It gave me an opportunity to find out what really happened to him, without my needing to visit that depressing small town where I'd met him or to actually see his all but empty cell-like adult day-care bedroom.

Some policemen found his body, almost covered by long, dead grass, just below the barn where he'd painted the "little girls"; he was curled on his left side, almost in a fetal position, with both hands covering his face, not unlike a cat at sleep or rest. Supposedly it was a heart attack, but that didn't account for the abrasions on his exposed face and hands; a rough, red, rash-like disruption on his flesh, which was eventually dismissed as fire-ant bites. Nor did the "official" cause of death account for the blissful look on his face that the policeman in one A&E special described; you don't have to be a doctor to know that some heart attacks are painful.

Nor do you need to be an expert on cats—especially *big* cats—to know what a cat's tongue can do to unprotected flesh, especially when they get it into their heads to keep licking and licking while snuggled together in a pile of warm, furry flesh.

Maybe Hobart Gurney didn't mean to say good-bye *per se* during that self-prescribed tour of his creations; maybe he'd just grown nostalgic after seeing the pictures I'd given to him. Funny how he took the album with him, when he'd never forgotten a single cat he'd created, but then again, no one will ever know what drove him to turn a Depression-era job taken despite an aversion to heights into something more than his life's work. Perhaps *my* decision to collect photographs of his work ultimately led to his death, which I heard about on the CNN news. But if that is so, I can't quite feel guilty about it—after all, Gurney hadn't painted cats in years; true, nothing stopped him from painting them on canvas, but I don't think that was Gurney's way at all.

Hadn't he said that what he was doing was work, something he was supposed to be doing? I doubt that the notion of painting for himself applied to his practical mind, just as I doubt that he could have foreseen a day when his cats would be severed from the very barns on which they lived, to be taken in wall-size chunks and "domesticated" in museums and art galleries all over the country.

Or...maybe he *did* have an inkling of what would happen, and knew that he wouldn't have his cats to himself for very much longer....

And, considering what was written on his tombstone—by whom, I don't know—I don't think I'm the only person who *maybe* knows what really happened to Hobart Gurney, down in the long, dead, flattened grass below the "little girls"...for this is what is carved on his barn-gray tombstone:

> No Heaven will not ever Heaven be,
> Unless my Cats are there to Welcome me.

All I can say is, I hope it was warm, and soft, and *loving*, there in the long, dead grass, with the little girls....

In Memory of:

Beanie, Ming, Fella, Ollie, Stan, Puddin', Blackie, Cupcake, Smokie, Prissy, Mish-Mish, Dewie, Rusty, Precious, Puff, Lucky, Eric, Sweetheart, Jack Early Gray, Charlie, Dolly, Maynard, Willie, Gwen, Laya, Spunky, Belle, Stripes, Book, Moo-Moo, Bruiser, Monkey, Goldie, Poco, Butterball, Spooky, Silky, Ladybug, Orangey, Ko-Ko, Frosty, Simba, Rosie,

Mrs. T., Mister, Muffin (Bubba), Speedy, Whiskers,
Bitsy, Purr-Bear, Kay-Tu, Chloe, Bippy, Brutis, Teddy,
Amelia, Elmo, Alphie, Gloria, Woody, Jezebel, Tigger,
Pansy, Oscar, April, Peokoe, Meg, Adrian, Sylvester,
Baby, Marco Polo, Lovey, Candy, Lola, Lacy, Poopie
(Violet), Queenie, Otto, Babykins, Momma Cat, Cutie
Pie, Sandy, Beauty, Sean, Chewie, Scooter, Mittens,
Taffy, Boo Boo, Clyde, Bailey, Gummitch, Dundee,
Chatty, Princess, Pinky, Apollo, Amber, Denise,
Callie, Bijou, Squeeky, Cee-Cee, Felix, Boogie, Little
Boy, Sugarplum, Tweetie Pie, Ruby, Penny, Fluffy (II),
Pumpkin, Casper, Boots, Jet, Honey, Beau, Angel,
Mack, Bugsy, Miss Kitty, Katie, June Bug, Cinnamon,
Tippi, Gracie, Quinn, Grady, Trudy, Baby Biscuit,
Max (and) Mongo, Ebony, Graykins, Fluffer-Nutter,
The Dude, Harley, Inky, Bogie, and Chickpea.

AFTERWORD

Hobart Gurney's real-life alter-ego, a man named Harley Warrick, 76, passed away November 24, 2000, after a lifetime spent painting over 20,000 barns within a fifty-five-year period—while he painted the same slogan "Chew Mail Pouch Tobacco. Treat Yourself to the Best" on every one of those barns, other painters have made forays into mural-type barn art, but none of them ever did so on the sheer scale or volume which can be credited to Mr. Warrick. When I first saw a TV feature on his work, done when he was still alive, I immediately came up with the idea for this story. Everything literally fell into place while I was watching that short featurette. In the Midwest, where I've lived most of my life, barn paintings aren't uncommon, and many of them feature animals—including the occasional cat.

The cats in this story, the ones Gurney painted, and loved, and eventually chose to die with, are all based on my own cats, some of whom are still alive, most of whom are gone. I wish I could have fit in descriptions of all of them, the ones who are no longer here, but the story *was* about Mr. Gurney. I also wish I had more than photographs of those cats, but aside from my memories of them, those pictures are all that *is* left of too many lives, too many sweet cats who all too briefly shared their lives with mine. Once I'm gone, even the pictures will lose their meaning, reduced to deteriorating pigment on chemically-treated paper, augmented by some names written on the back of each print. Like Mr. Gurney, I wish I could make myself small enough to curl up with my cats; I can't think of anything better when it comes to dying. But, like Mr. gurney, at least I've tried to create something of a written record of my cats, fragmentary and as ultimately useless in the cosmic scale of what is or isn't truly remarkable as it may be. I've put a few of my cats into my work, sometimes under their own names, occasionally under their "second" names (something I now regret, since those cats deserved their time in the spotlight, too, so no one will automatically know, for example, that the three cats mentioned in my first published novelette, "Four Days Before the Snow," were really my Tigger, Jezebel and Muffin, and not

Digger, Pooter and Shmoo), but I've had so many more cats than I've written stories, and there's no way to fit them all in. I only had some of them for days; strays I took in sometimes died quickly, due to past neglect no amount of food, love or medicine could negate. Others, I had long enough to miss so badly the very thought of them makes me break down, crying. No matter how often I may write about them, or try to describe them, nothing will—nothing can—bring any of them back.

That's why, when this story was first published, I was heartbroken when the printer accidentally left off about one third of the names originally listed at the end of the story. There was no way to add them on, and since the story didn't make the cut for *The Year's Best Fantasy & Horror* that following year, there was no way to fix the printer's error. Those names are back place, and sadly augmented by many more. Fourteen of those names represent cats and kittens of mine who died within a seventeen-day period in 1998, after an epidemic of dry form FIP. That was an abysmal time for me, which was exacerbated less than a month later when someone whom I thought was a friend— and fellow cat-lover—sent me a Xmas card (I don't dare call it a Christmas card) depicting hands rising up from a graveyard, reaching for a horrific "Santa," followed by the interior inscription "Not a creature was stirring." As if I wasn't aware of *that*, after I'd spent a little over two weeks dealing with up to three deaths a day. Why that person chose to pull such a stunt, I have no idea, but it did make me realize that there's no guarantee that anything I write about my cats will actually affect anyone at all...but yet, considering the options for anyone else even remembering these animals at all, in any context, I still try to work them in. And while I seldom re-read my own work, unlike Mr. Gurney visiting his barn-cats, I still remember those cats. Every one of them. Sometimes I forget the exact day when some of them died, while other deaths are frozen in my memory due to them happening on holidays, or other key days in my life, but they all mattered to me.

Even if their lives didn't impact the world in any significant way.

And even if their names are nothing more than a listing of words at the end of a story only a few people out of the billions in the world might ever read.

They all mattered to me.

* * * * * * *

In the years since I wrote the above Afterword, my own life has come to mirror that of Mr. Gurney— thanks to the ubiquitous usage of computers and email to conduct to conduct virtually all submissions to just about every magazine and anthology out there, I'm no longer able to pursue my life's work—just as poor Mr. Gurney was squeezed out of his occupation by old age and an inability to climb those ladders. Yet another irony, a foreseeing of my own career's demise in my own work....

As if losing my cats one by one wasn't enough of a loss. Well, at least I had a chance to share my meager abilities before my own disabilities rendered me liter-ally literarily obsolete. My cats don't care....

UNIVERSES

She was little more than a soft shape,
clinging to the concrete on First Street North,
frost-glued and unmoving,
save for the faint ripple of fur where
the icy breeze stroked her.
A calico kitten, maybe three-four months old,
car-hit,
disemboweled,
front paws neatly crossed,
eyes shut as if in sleep, pink-tinged lips
upcurled in a secret cat-smile.
At home, my Penny and Heidi were of the same age,
the same rough size, only better-fed,
and alive and warm, still curled in my unmade bed.
How long *she* had been there, I couldn't tell—
her spilled insides were stuck to the street,
resisting my efforts to move her,
but her body was still soft to my probing fingers,
her fur still silky,
white with daubs of orange and grey.
She could have been a playmate for my kittens,
I thought as I cried, tears pooling

along the lower rims of my glasses,
while I searched the pre-dawn back alleys
for a scrap of board,
something to scrape her off the street,
while the image of her torn insides
warred with her frozen, enigmatic smile.
Cardboard in hand,
I cried as I struggled to pry her off the street;
Bits of her shell-pink intestines,
some of her fur remained,
a soft shadow,
as I started to slide her into the crinkly white
plastic shopping bag I'd been carrying that morning—
until I paused to take one last look at
the kitten whose life I'd never share,
even as a blur of white-orange-grey
glimpsed running away from me down some alley…
and I noticed how the spirals of her
eviscerated insides resembled a conch shell's
inner secret spiral,
or the smaller spring-twist of life,
of the DNA chain,
and in the grey, cold time between running time
and eternal cessation,
I realized that this was *her* time of sharing,
her last gift to whichever human found her
after another human had killed her—
Never again could I look at my cats,
my babies,
as little more than furry bodies,

never again;
not after witnessing the tender universe
of inner being,
the fragile, all-too-easily revealed
mainspring of life once lived.
As I gently folded her into the bag,
I, too,
managed to find my sad, secret smile.

AFTERWORD

The events described in this poem really did happen to me, over twenty years ago; I was beyond heartbroken when I found that little kitten that early morning, because she was so warm: she had to have been hit after I'd gone on my daily looking-for-aluminum-cans run. I'd missed her life, but her death has stayed with me for over two decades.

The other kittens mentioned, Penny and Heidi, are both long gone, but before she died, Penny did manage to help save my life—when my house was filling up with carbon monoxide, and I was going in and out of consciousness, she sat on my chest and swatted my face with her paws, which let me know that despite my actually being sick with the flu, what I was experiencing (a horrible headache, nausea, and muscle aches) was far more than the flu bug. If it hadn't have been for her whacking at my face with her paw, I might not have made it.

This poem was first published in 1993, in an unapproved, variant visual form which turned a piece of poetry into a four-paragraph mini-story, with multiple typos and incorrect spellings; this current form is my approved format for this work....

ACKNOWLEDGMENTS

"The Hemingway Kittens" originally appeared in *Shelf Life: Fantastic Stories Celebrating Bookstores*, edited by Gary Ketter, Dreamhaven, 2002. Copyright © 2002, 2013 by A. R. Morlan.

"Cat in the Box" appeared on the Sci-Fi.com/ Scifiction website in April, 2001. Copyright © 2002, 2013 by A. R. Morlan.

"…And Mongo Was His Name-O" is published here for the first time. Copyright © 2013 by A. R. Morlan.

"The Cat Tracker Lady of Asad Alley" is published here for the first time. Copyright © 2013 by A. R. Morlan.

"The Cat with the Tulip Face" originally appeared in *Short Story Paperbacks*, #29, 1991, and was also collected in *Ewerton Death Trip: A Walk Through the Dark Side of Town*, by A. R. Morlan, Borgo Press, 2011. Copyright © 1991, 2011, 2013 by A. R. Morlan.

"A Little Pinch Is All You Need" appeared in *New Blood*, Fall, 1988. Copyright © 1988, 2013 by A. R. Morlan.

"Hunger" originally appeared in *Night Terrors*, #3, 1997, and was also collected in *Ewerton Death Trip: A*

ABOUT THE AUTHOR

A. R. Morlan was born in Chicago, IL on January 3, 1958, and moved with her family to the Los Angeles area in 1961, where she lived until 1969, when her family moved to Wisconsin, where she still lives.

Morlan has a BS degree in English (Liberal Arts), *Magna Cum Laude*, from the now defunct Mount Senario College in Ladysmith, Wisconsin, which folded shortly before a F3 tornado tore apart her town of residence in 2002. She has been a free-lance writer since 1983, and has had fiction and non-fiction published in over 130 different magazines, anthologies, collections, and e-zines in the US, Canada and parts of Europe, in addition to two novels, *The Amulet* and *Dark Journey* (both available from Borgo Press), a Romanian-language collection called *Femia Coperta* (Cover Woman) which came out in 2004, a co-edited (with Martin H. Greenberg) anthology called *Zodiac Fantastic* (DAW, 1997), and assorted introductions for various short fiction collections by other authors. Her collections for Borgo Press include: *The Chimera and the Shadowfox Griefer and Other Curious People*, *Ewerton Death Trip: A Walk Through the Dark Side of*

Town, The Fold-O-Rama Wars at the Blue Moon Roach Hotel and Other Colorful Tales of Transformation and Tattoos, Of Vampires and Gentlemen: Tales of Erotic Horror, and *'Rillas and Other Science Fiction Stories,* plus other volumes yet forthcoming.

She is single and childless, but a proud pet-parent of a varying number of cat-children.